DAMASCUS ROAD

*Julie —
Never give up
on your dreams!
Have a great future!*

DAMASCUS ROAD

R. Louis Costley III
with Greg Meeker

TATE PUBLISHING & *Enterprises*

Tate Publishing
& Enterprises

Damascus Road

Copyright © 2006 by R. Louis Costley III. All rights reserved.

No part of this publication may be reproduced, stored in a retrieval system or transmitted in any way by any means, electronic, mechanical, photocopy, recording or otherwise without the prior permission of the author except as provided by USA copyright law.

All scripture quotations are taken from the Holy Bible, New Living Translation, Copyright © 1996. Used by permission of Tyndale House Publishers, Inc. All rights reserved.

I AM

Music and lyrics by Mark Hoffman. Used by permission. All rights reserved.

This novel is a work of fiction. However, several names, descriptions, entities and incidents included in the story are based on the lives of real people.

Book design copyright © 2006 by Tate Publishing, LLC. All rights reserved.
Cover design by Lynly Taylor
Interior design by Jennifer Redden

Published in the United States of America

ISBN: 1-5988676-6-0
06.10.17

You will hear of wars and rumors of wars, but see to it that you are not alarmed. Such things must happen, but the end is still to come. Nation will rise against nation, and kingdom against kingdom. All these are the beginning of birth pains.

Matthew 24:6–8

PROLOGUE

The illusion, a pool of water floating above the desert floor, formed a translucent, wavy barrier between what was clearly seen, and that which was not; a contrast of refreshing coolness in the midst of extreme heat.

Paul ignored the illusion, though, as he ran forward in urgent desperation, more aware, instead, of the pounding of his heart within his chest. Constricting with every breath, the muscles in his throat began to rob him of much needed oxygen, and the heat emanating from the arid soil caused his lungs to burn like fire. If that wasn't bad enough, the soles of his feet were blistering inside his high-tech running shoes, as each jarring step swallowed yet another cubic inch of sand. The jeans he was wearing impeded every stride he took, slowing his progress forward to what seemed a snail's pace. His red T-shirt was soaked in sweat, as was the bandana covering his head. He continued to push his pace, reaching deep within to find that intestinal fortitude his father so often spoke of as he was growing up. Adorned in black riding gloves, his hands and arms pumped like pistons. The hunting knife in its sheath rattled and slapped his thigh, while the gun holstered to his left side pierced the muscle tissue between his ribs.

Suddenly, his body coiled in pain as a cramp formed in his gut, and he came to an abrupt stop, wheezing and gasping for air.

Though in better shape than most men his age, his body was now betraying him.

The mirrored, black-framed sunglasses covered his eyes as they darted back and forth, scanning the blazing surroundings with fatal urgency. The shades also exaggerated the sweat flowing from his forehead. Blood was trickling from his nose and the corner of his mouth. His thoughts were racing out of control, rational and irrational, swirling together in a vortex of panic and fear; yet, he was keenly focused on the single, primary task of getting away. Quickly glancing behind, his gaze locked onto the mass of small figures, warped and distorted by the waves of rising heat, moving in his direction.

Any irrational thoughts he may have entertained were immediately dismissed as the internal drive for self-preservation... to survive... regained control, and he took off once again. No matter how fast he ran, the mass of figures grew larger as they began to close the gap. Outfitted much differently than Paul, they were better suited to their more primitive surroundings, and apparently more prepared for this method of pursuit. Swords brandished and shields ready, they ran in unison... and tired slowly. Paul looked back again to see them closing in on him, and realized just how much out of his element he really was. How is it possible, he thought, that Roman soldiers would be chasing him? Without warning, he tripped and stumbled to the desert surface. Rolling over, he glanced back again to see the Romans bearing down on him. Scrambling to his feet, he lunged forward in a sprint for his life. He could hear the sound of the soldier's armor behind him, and reached even deeper to find the strength to keep going, and then fell again... a bad fall...

✳✳✳

It was the fall that woke him up with a start. It always did. His sweating and heavy breathing were real enough, but his gaze now brought into view the walls, familiar shadows, and furnishings of his own bedroom. Realizing that he had been dreaming—that same dream—Paul climbed out of bed and headed to the bathroom.

His initial thought, at first glance in the mirror, was that he looked beat-up, like in his dream. Turning on the water at the sink, he cupped his hands under the spout and allowed the bowl they formed to fill up. The cold splash of H20 on his face brought to him a strange sort of comfort. He was no longer in a land not his own, but was back in familiar territory.

I'm home, he thought, as he glanced back into the mirror.

Then reality set in, and he wondered if that dream of his might not actually be a better place.

"Whatever," he spoke softly to himself, closing the door to attend to more pressing issues.

STEVE

The saddlebags, rifle holster, and hydration sacks gave the appearance of a tireless, loyal, and powerful old-west horse. If not for the chrome and modern trappings, Paul thought, it might as well be just that. Snapping his rifle into the holster, donning his black riding gloves, and climbing aboard the mechanical beast, he wondered if this was what it really felt like to be a gunslinger of western yore.

Pulling his helmet down over his hair and eyes, those thoughts quickly dissipated from his mind, giving way to the realization that no old-time gunslinger had *this* kind of gear. His motorcycle itself was enough to make that crystal clear—a built-for-speed monster of a bike with a cutting-edge array of defenses, and a top speed that would leave anything coming after him in the dust.

"On," he spoke cryptically. All nostalgia ran for cover as the visor in his helmet glided down over his eyes into the groove of its frame just below his nose. A cushioned flap slid out from under the front of his helmet to form a secure fit beneath his chin, and his motorcycle started automatically, with the low rumbling "purr" of a wild Bengal tiger. Revving up the motor with a few twists of the accelerator handle, Paul adjusted the helmet's night-sight, infrared detection and computer readout.

Backing out of his driveway, he stared down the road that lay in front of him.

"This ain't no ten-gallon hat," he mumbled to himself in a bad Texas accent, bringing a smile to his face, and a whimsical exhortation of his "horse" to get moving with a gentle pat on the back seat of the bike.

"Gid'yup," Paul joked to himself, his trusty old mount responding obediently to the flick of his wrist and twist of the accelerator. Launching forward, 179 racing thoroughbreds catapulted man and machine into the darkened hours of early morning. Ten seconds, and a quarter mile later, he rounded the bow at the end of his street and headed out toward the open road.

The night-sight of Paul's helmet turned the road before him into day, and he could see everything as if the sun was, indeed, standing at high noon. Immediately he became aware of the gas gauge transposed before his eyes, hovering just a hair above empty.

"Nope. You ain't no hay-eatin' horse, that's for sure," he thought out loud, scanning the horizon for the nearest convenient store. Up the road about a mile was the Qwik Mart, he remembered, as he set his mind to the task of feeding his beast.

There was something else he spotted up the road that caught his attention. Actually, *someone* else, with much the same build as Paul, around thirty with long blonde hair, but carrying a backpack like some college geek.

No way, he thought, realizing a deep familiarity with the person as he passed him by. He slowed down and pulled off to the side of the road, turning the bike around to catch a glimpse of the person from the front.

"Zoom," he spoke into his helmet, and the figure doubled in size in Paul's visor. He knew this guy.

"Steve?"

Steve seemed a bit unsettled by the sudden interest from Paul, but nodded his head in recognition as he continued to walk steadily toward the store. Paul tore a quick 180-degree turn, spewing rock and gravel behind him. Arriving at the store, he pulled into a space reserved for motorcycles, reached over to his left and extracted a half-inch fuel line from a two-foot tall box. He inserted the end into a matching hole on top of his fuel tank, and waved his left palm across the scanner on top of the box. About five seconds later, the tank was filled with pressurized natural gas, and the box beeped at him. He unplugged the line, and it retracted back into its holding position in the fuel pump. Hopping off the bike, he took another look back at Steve, still about a hundred yards or so away. Turning, Paul headed toward the Qwik Mart entrance.

"Off," he spoke, stepping up to the front doors, and the motorcycle shut down immediately. At the same time, the visor on his helmet glided up, and the flap slid from under his chin back up into the lower front of his helmet.

"Alarm," he commanded, and the bike became accessible only to someone willing to carry it. Without Paul's own voice command, the machine would never start again.

Entering the store, he turned to the newspaper stand that was just inside the front doors. As Steve was nearing the street entrance to the parking lot, he took off his helmet, and laid it beside the paper rack. He picked up a paper and began to read—or, rather, made believe he was reading—the front page of the news. Standing as non-chalantly as he could, he watched over the top edge of the paper, through the front window, as Steve made his way across the parking lot.

Approaching the entrance, Steve glanced over at Paul's motorcycle, then up at Paul through the window. Once inside, he hesitated at the doors, then walked over to the newspapers and looked down, glancing at the headlines. He stood there next to Paul, unsure of whether he should say anything or not. After what seemed like an eternity, Paul looked up from "reading" his paper, and they just looked into each other's eyes.

"Paul," Steve said with a slight nod.

"Steve," responded Paul, monotone and dry. He gave Steve a quick up-and-down look, then asked, "When did you get back?"

"Couple of days ago. I'm… uh… still waiting on my stuff." Now it was Steve's turn to pause and look Paul over. Finally, he said, "Long time, eh?"

"Not long enough, Steve," Paul said in a voice laced with deep sarcasm. There was another awkward moment of silence.

"Yeah, well," Steve finally replied, "I gotta do some shopping." He moved past Paul toward the food and beverage items.

Paul gave a disgusted smirk that Steve didn't see, and went back to his paper.

Steve wandered about the store, shopping for what looked like a week's worth of stuff—soda, bread, ham, cheese, cookies, chips, a gallon of milk, toilet paper, and every package of Ho-Ho's in stock.

The clerk behind the counter watched him with amusement. An older, larger woman she was, whose dark-circled, baggy eyes spoke volumes about her life outside the confines of the store. She'd seen him in there on several occasions recently, each time loading up on just about everything a Qwik Mart could offer the discerning bachelor.

Finally, he made his way up to the register and laid everything on the counter. "Hi there," he greeted her with a wink.

"Well, hi there." The clerk began scanning the items. "You're becoming quite the regular in here."

"Yes, ma'am, you know how it is… decent service, good prices." He smiled at her again, and then admitted, "Easy to walk to."

The clerk laughed out loud at the confession as she rang up the last item. "Now *that* I believe," she concurred. "Will that be all this morning?"

"No, ma'am," he said, extracting a rose from the fresh flower display on the counter. "One of these, too."

"For the little sweetheart?"

"Sort of." He handed her the rose. "For you."

The clerk's face immediately turned a deep pink, and Steve thought for a fraction of a second that she was going to cry. "Oh, thank you. How sweet." It was easy to see that kindness like this seldom ever came her way.

"You're always smiling, and very nice to me," Steve responded, feeling a bit embarrassed himself. "Makes me feel good… just my way of saying thanks."

"Ohhhh." The clerk smiled

"So, what do I owe you?" Steve asked.

The clerk, smelling the rose with a joy not felt in a long time, told him, "Nothing. It's on me."

"Forget it," he protested, "There's a lot of stuff here."

"Hey, it's worth every penny," she protested even more, looking him straight in the eyes. "I'll show my bingo friends the rose that a good-looking, hunk-of-a-younger-man gave me."

She flashed the most satisfied of grins. "They'll envy me for months."

Steve smiled back at her, understanding that he had truly made her night.

"Hey, if that's the case," he said, pointing to the refrigerator with the sandwiches, "throw in a couple of those subs."

"I'm afraid that'll take a *dozen* roses," she said with a wink.

They both laughed robustly, as Steve grabbed his bag and began to walk away.

"Well, good night," he said, and then caught himself with a small chuckle, "I mean, morning. Have a good morning... and thanks a lot."

"No," she said half-defiantly, as she smelled the fragrance of the rose again, "thank *you*. And you have a good *morning*, yourself."

Steve slowly made his way over to stand next to Paul. He picked up a paper without much intent on reading it, but pretended to do so anyway.

Paul hesitated a moment, then without looking at him asked in a sardonic tone, "Why'd you come back?"

"I had to. This is my home."

Paul could no longer keep his sense of betrayal hidden. "Then why'd you leave in the first place? I mean, Jesus Christ, Steve..."

The tension was thick as they stood for a moment, staring one at the other, each groping for the right words to say. Finally, Steve shrugged and said, "Forget it. You wouldn't understand."

"Look, Steve... you just up and left," Paul said, the anger in his voice escalating a bit. "No goodbye, no explanation, nothing. When the fire got hot, you split."

Steve felt very much on his heels. "I had to leave. I had to get away from here. Too much was happening, too many people were getting hurt. I was losing it, man. My mind… my heart—"

Paul would have none of it. "I stayed, Luc stayed—"

"Aw, come on, man," Steve interrupted, no longer just defending himself, but making a case for his choices and actions. "Look at you," he said, staring over at Paul's bike, "the 'Rebel with a cause.' I was never like you, Paul, and you know that. I couldn't do it anymore. I'm just a simple man—"

Paul interrupted Steve, now, finishing his sentence. "Who *runs* from adversity! Innocent people needed you. They counted on you and you ran out on them."

"Killing is killing," Steve countered. "Good guys, bad guys… it doesn't matter. It's all the same, bro. But, there's a better way, Paul. A much better way."

There was a long, uncomfortable pause, during which both Paul and Steve took a deep breath and let their anger subside.

"We were best friends, Steve. Remember? I got your back, you got mine. But, instead, you left me carrying the cross."

"I ran out of options, Paul," Steve said pleadingly. "My… my soul… was crying out for freedom." He took another long look at Paul's motorcycle. "I was a slave to that vicious war of hate." He moved his gaze to Paul. "Just like you; but, not anymore, bro. I'm taking a different path now, carrying a different cross, and I'm *never* turning back."

Again, the tension of silence hung like a thick fog between them, and they looked at each other for a few seconds.

Finally, Steve broke the silence. "Well, I gotta go."

He extended his hand out to Paul, who first looked at it, then into his eyes, and took it in what was far from a friendly handshake.

"It's good to see you again, Paul. I'll see you around."

"Yeah," was Paul's only response.

Steve turned to leave, getting halfway to the doors, then stopped and turned to look back at Paul. "By the way, I got me a club outside of town on Damascus Road. Come on out sometime." He smiled. "Never a cover." He reached into his backpack, pulled out a CD and paperback novel, and was looking at them. "I've got some friends in a band. They did a CD dedicated to the club and its future. One of them wrote a novel, too." He handed them to Paul. "Check 'em out. Being a drummer," he said with a smile, "I think you'll dig the music. They're both pretty good, actually."

Paul forced a smile of his own, unable to mask the disappointment inside his heart. "Yeah, sure. I'll do that sometime." He went back to "reading" his paper. "See ya 'round, Steve."

Picking up on Paul's dismissive tone, Steve left the store. Walking past the motorcycle, he took another glance at it, and then looked over his shoulder to catch a glimpse of Paul staring at him through the window.

Paul watched him as he walked away, then looked at the store clerk, who was lost in the aroma of her rose. He thought to himself that he, or anyone else for that matter, could walk out with the whole store and she would still be standing there just smelling her rose. For a fleeting moment, the memory of Steve's tender nature filled his mind. That was, after all, what drew him close to Steve in the first place. *Typical,* he thought, as he took a final look at Steve crossing the parking lot. Then the anger and disappointment flooded his mind once again. He shrugged it off, shook his head in disgust, and went back to his newspaper. Actually reading it this time, he started, and finished, with the funnies. It wasn't long before the clerk came back to reality long enough to flash a "this isn't a library" look in Paul's direction. Taking the hint, he tossed the paper down and exited the Qwik Mart.

He jumped on his mechanical steed and sat there for a moment looking at the CD and book Steve had given him. The front picture was of a mountain range, with a tornado and storm to the upper left of the hills, and a beautiful, peaceful sunrise to the right. A road ran up the middle of the picture, and forked at the mountains. One road went to the left, toward the storm, and the other to the right, in front of the mountains, toward the sunset. The word "Damascus" was embedded in the mountains themselves, as was the word "Road" in the path heading toward the sunset. Below the path to the left were the words, "The end," and under the one to the right, the words "... and a new beginning"...

Damascus Road
The end... and a new beginning

Pretty cool, he thought, as he opened the CD case, retrieved the disc, and inserted it into the player installed on his motor. He then stuffed the case and the novel into a pocket inside his jacket. The first song that kicked in was a funky, hard-driven rock song, laced with heavy bass guitar and rhythm guitars. And it *rocked*.

With that as his ticket, he departed from the parking lot, dispensing with his frustrations and anger by leaving as much rubber on the road as possible. Listening to the song from the CD, he cruised the highway, and found himself lost in the music and the words...

Changes are'a comin'
I feel it in the air
People living life deep in despair.
Things are gonna happen
Like we've never seen before
And man won't survive without the Lord.

> *Ushering in*
> > *a new way of life.*
> *Bringing to end*
> > *all world strife.*
> *Coming in glory*
> > *at an unknown time.*
> *Don't turn your back,*
> > *don't get left behind.*

Paul was intrigued. It was as if the song was written for him, personally, and spoke deeply to the very circumstances he found himself embroiled in. His conversation with Steve came to mind, and the very words of this song seemed to be saying the same thing he alluded to back at the store. Memories of the conversations he used to overhear his parents have with their friends from church infiltrated his thoughts, and he found himself paying closer attention to the song than the road he was traveling…

> *You better get ready*
> *Start lookin' for the signs*
> *Famine, disease, and war until his time.*
> *Now don't get worried.*
> *These things have got to come.*
> *A new day dawned*
> > *with the rise of the Son.*

Damascus Road

Ushering in
  a new way of life.
Bringing to end
  all world strife.
Coming in glory
  at an unknown time.
Don't turn your back,
  don't get left behind.

THOUGHTS

He didn't know it then, but his life was about to change. Not that his life was normal or ordinary, 'cause it wasn't. Nobody's was anymore, for that matter; but, this was different, a change that would cut straight through to his heart. At first it was just a feeling... a gnawing feeling. Y'know, the kind that just sits there in your chest, growing with every breath you take until you can't think straight. Sure, everyone goes through changes eventually, but what ever happened to those nice, quiet walks in the park?

WAKE UP, DUDE !

The sun was barely cracking the eastern horizon as Paul arrived at the warehouses—a meandering conglomeration of abandoned buildings that had long ago seen their prime. Winding his motorcycle through the maze of small alleyways, he pulled up in front of his unit. With a swing of his right leg over the rear of his cycle, he audibly "alarmed" it, then made his way to the garage door that was the front entrance. He shook the fence of steel bars that secured his home away from home, and then pulled out a set of keys to unlock it.

Sliding the fence from left to right, he proceeded to unlock the garage door, and then pulled it above his head to reveal what could only be described as an old-time hippy hangout. The floor and walls were covered with carpet, a multi-colored patchwork of thick shag that spanned the spectrum of a rainbow. Some used furniture made the room look comfortable—a couch and chairs, a coffee table, and a refrigerator, all of them having seen a lot of use. Near the back of the warehouse were the makings of a band set-up—a drum set, some speakers, a stereo system, and several guitar stands.

Paul quickly made himself at home, going straight to the fridge for a drink, and then turned on the stereo while taking a seat behind the drums. He ignored the music on the stereo, and began to play a little bit on his kit. How he used to love to play music with his brother, he thought to himself. Of course, thinking about it sapped him of the desire to play the drums any more, so he just put the sticks back in their bag and leaned back against the wall. His eyes closed, absorbed in the music from the stereo, he sipped on his drink.

Suddenly, in rhythm with the music, he heard what sounded like a foot tapping to the beat. Slowly opening his eyes, he saw two men standing at the entrance of the warehouse. Silhouetted against the backdrop of the still rising sun, his bike behind them, one of them was indeed tapping his foot.

Paul could still see enough of the men in the sun's glare to see they each had heavy, electro-pulse machine guns resting on their shoulders. The guy that was tapping his foot stopped abruptly, and addressed Paul directly.

"Where you been, Pauly," he asked with mock, sarcastic concern. "Tony's been worried about you."

"Go away," Paul muttered, feigning sleep, "can't you see I'm sleeping?"

The other gunman began laughing maniacally, and then stopped only to swing the weapon from his shoulder to waist-high, aimed straight at Paul. "Wake up, dude," he yelled, laughing once again.

His partner quickly joined him, leveling his own gun, and they unloaded their weapons on the walls, furniture, music equipment, and windows. The sound was deafening, and the destruction put out by the high-tech guns was impressive. The moment was not lost on the gunmen, who found great joy and humor at the damage they wielded.

"It's a beautiful day in the neighborhood," the first one sang in a mock Mr. Rodgers tone, his laughter cutting off the macabre melody.

The second gunman quickly picked up on the tune. "Hey… won't *you* be… my neighbor?" he said sappily, pointing at Paul and laughing uncontrollably. Both men took one last look at their handiwork, and then ran off, still laughing and singing their own fractured version of the Mr. Rodgers theme song.

Paul stayed huddled on the floor until he was sure they were gone. Having experienced this same kind of wake-up call in the past, he instinctively dove to the ground a split second before the shooting began, covering his head with his arms. Like the times before, Paul was never shot at directly. But he was also never sure if the day would come that Tony would finally send the Reaper along for the ride.

He slowly lifted his head to peruse the damage, his ears still ringing from the noise, his body weary as the adrenaline rush began to wear off. The familiar harmony of sirens that accompanied these early morning song and dance routines pierced the distant air. It all seemed so convenient, he thought, that the cops were always at the ready for these shows, as if they were forewarned of the coming event.

"I should have stayed in bed," he muttered, gingerly picking himself off the ground to head outside the warehouse and wait.

For the *real* show to begin.

BILLY

To Paul, it seemed to be a bit of overkill, with a half-dozen or so police cars forming a perimeter barricade around his warehouse. After all, it wasn't the first time this had happened—and probably wouldn't be the last. Their sirens had been turned off, thankfully, but the whirling and flashing of their lights was quite the nuisance. The cacophony of radio chatter between the cars and their dispatchers only made the throbbing in his head more acute.

As usual, Billy was the first one to arrive, and he surveyed the scene through his over-sized Ray Ban aviators, which, like today, always seemed to have a fingerprint smudged on at least one of the expensive lenses. He was tall and semi-fit, consistent with the level of middle management he had achieved on the force. He and Paul went back many years, to their high school days, and although they were not exactly friends, they maintained a semblance of civility between them. Billy's daily regimen of fast food, store-bought pastries, pizza, brew—or any other domestic charcuteries that would fit in his hand—were beginning to betray his undersized shirt that was bulging at the buttons. No matter the season, he sweat like a pig. There was a definite cause and effect relationship between the can ring imprinted on his back pocket, the bulge in his lower lip, and the dark yellow tone of his uneven teeth that jutted out every time he grinned. One look at him and the word "redneck" came to mind, and his boisterous East Texas drawl only reinforced that image.

He truly seemed bored listening to Paul tell him the all-too-familiar events that took place just moments earlier. As they spoke, two sports cars were speeding up the winding gravel drive that led to the group of buildings. He recognized both vehicles immediately. The first one, a teal Corvette, belonged to Luc, a medium-built black man about the same age as Paul, who was Paul's second in command. The second, a beautiful blue Mustang GT with two white racing stripes that ran the length of the vehicle, was the possession of Mark, a tall and slender Asian man in his mid-twenties. Both of them were part of the group Paul commanded, and were always at his beck-and-calling. The urgency of their arrival engulfed the crowd in a cloud of dust, resulting in a *second* cloud of coughing and verbal obscenities from the deputies. Immediately the passenger door on the Mustang swung open. Stepping out of the car and running toward them was Missy, a young, petite and beautiful dark-haired woman.

"Y'know, one day I'm gonna have to tell your sister, there, that she ain't got a brother no more," Billy said, acknowledging the new arrivals to the scene.

"She understands," Paul replied with arms folded, sunglasses looking past Billy with dismissive indifference.

"Ya have to stop this, Paul. There ain't nothin' you can do. Can't ya see that? It's out'a yer control."

"I gotta do what I gotta do, Billy. Besides, you're not doing anything to stop all this."

Billy's immediate mock defensiveness was almost humorous. "We do what we can, ya know that."

"Sometimes I wonder about that."

The tension was threatening to escalate, but it was Missy who cut the cord stretching between them.

"Paul!" she exclaimed as she ran up and hugged him. "Oh, God, Paul, are you okay?"

She looked up at him, her deep blue eyes in stark contrast to Paul's brown, then pulled away to inspect him for any obvious damage.

"Yeah, sis… I'm fine—"

"Fer now," Billy interjected, staring straight into Paul's shades. "But if he keeps this up, he won't be." Then he addressed Missy, "appreciating" her beauty a little too obviously. "You be sure to tell him that whenever you see him."

Paul casually stepped between Billy and his sister, as he replied in his own exaggerated Texas accent. "Now, Billy… that sure don't sound t'me like you're concerned fer my safety."

Billy's ire was certainly aroused by Paul's obvious mocking, and he stared at him with rage in his eyes. He was about to let into Paul, when he realized that all eyes were on *him*, and quickly backed off.

"Well, I got all I need. Y'all be careful now," he said, tilting his head to the left to get a quick glance at Paul's sister. "You look real nice today, Missy."

"Thanks, Billy," she said, as he turned to go to his squad car. It wasn't long before all of the police cars cleared the warehouses, and there was time for everyone to gather their thoughts and take a collective sigh as they made their way inside the shot-up room.

Mark was the first one to speak. "That was a close one, Paul."

"*Too* close! You sure you're okay?" Luc concurred.

"Yeah. If they wanted me hurt or dead, I would be. Tony's

just letting me know he cares," Paul said jestfully, with no one else sharing his humor.

"Blood is thicker than water, eh?" Luc said sarcastically, as he and Mark both surveyed the room.

"He's a freakin' psycho!" Mark shouted.

"What can I say?" Paul said, shrugging his shoulders. He then turned his attention to Mark. "Can you get ahold of everyone and tell them to be here at, say, 11… no, make that noon."

Mark looked at his watch, not liking the short notice he was given. "I'll do my best."

"Tell them to break whatever plans they have," Paul added.

"You got it," Mark said, turning his attention to Missy. "I'll see you later, okay?"

"Okay," she said, touching his arm affectionately. "Bye."

LUC

Luc watched Mark leave, then looked at the room full circle again and shook his head. This thing going on between Paul and Tony was pretty bizarre, and he, for one, couldn't quite understand any of it.

They had all gone to the same high school together, although Luc was a few years behind Paul, in the same class as Tony. They never hung out with each other, and hardly even knew the others existed. Paul had a pretty cool reputation, though, as a hot musician, and was always hanging out with the best looking chicks in the school. Luc was a bit of a loner, and found much success in his own right, excelling at the kind of things that were considered "nerdy." That never bothered him; his room had been filled with trophies for chess and fencing, and he was pretty content with himself.

It wasn't until about three or so years prior, when all this terrorist stuff started happening, that they hooked up and became friends. Paul seemed to take so much of what was happening personally, and was tireless in trying to stop it all. Luc found that very inspiring, even when it became obsessive, so he made a point of sticking to Paul like glue. He knew that Paul's cavalier attitude about the violence and terror came from his knowing that someone, namely himself, always had his back.

Luc, on the other hand, always felt like they were living on borrowed time. He tried to make the most, and best, of that time by fighting against the very thing that had essentially taken his *own* life away. After all, *borrowed* time was better than no time at all.

His family was rather big, and he was the youngest of six boys; still, he never really fit into his deeply religious family, and when they were all killed in one of the first attacks that occurred, he found in Paul a brother, bound in the soul, that he never had growing up.

"Hey, Luc," Paul said, thrusting himself into the deep thoughts of his close friend, "Got a gig for you."

"Gig" usually meant something new and cool to Luc. "What do ya need," he said attentively.

"Can you use the com-link downstairs and find out everything you can about these attacks… when, where, why. There's got to be a trend in there somewhere. We already know *who's* doing this, and how, but Tony's always one step ahead of us, and we gotta figure out how to stop him."

Being the "nerd" he was, the com-link was one of Luc's favorite toys to play with. Paul always seemed to have the coolest technology at his disposal. "No prob, but what if someone's put a trace on that info? You know how it is these days."

"Not to worry, my friend," Paul reassured him with a sly grin. "I put a trace-lock on it last week."

"A trace lock? That's G-stuff, man! I don't know how you do it, Paul."

Ignoring the implied question, and the subject of his access to the newest technology altogether, Paul got Luc directly on task. "Can you get on that ASAP? We need as much info as possible by noon."

"I'm on it," Luc acknowledged, making his way around Missy

and heading toward the back left corner of the room. Wrapping his arms around Paul's neck and shoulders from behind as he passed, he leaned in close and whispered in his ear, "It's good to see you in one piece, bro."

Paul smiled sincerely at him. "Thanks, Luc."

Luc turned and headed for the door to the back room, carefully concealed behind the carpet hung on the walls. Instinctively, he looked over his shoulder to make sure nobody unwanted was paying attention to him, and he caught the eye of Paul once again. He gave Luc a slight upward nod, with that familiar half-smile on his face, and it took Luc back to the day he had decided to join up with Paul and his band of hopeless idealists.

It had only been a couple of weeks since his family was killed when their church was destroyed. Luc now found himself in the middle of Tony's thugs, being taunted and slapped around. He was never a physically dominant type of person, and usually avoided conflict for the sake of a peaceful alternative. He didn't understand what was happening these days, because, after all, he never really fit into his family's lifestyle, and seldom ever attended church with them. Being surrounded by Tony and his minions didn't make any sense to him.

Then, without any warning, like a badger set on fire, Paul leapt into the middle of it all, and in the span of about sixty seconds proceeded to beat the daylights out of a couple of the guys that had been working him over. It was pretty amazing the way Paul just put those guys to the ground. When the rest of them were about to jump into the melee, Tony put an immediate stop to the circus.

After they left, Paul and he were standing there by themselves. Paul looked at him with a slight smile, and gave him that same upward nod, then turned to walk away. Luc watched him walk away for a moment, and then quickly jogged over to catch up with him.

They've been together ever since.

Luc gathered his thoughts together, and looked into Paul's eyes. It was almost like the two of them were remembering the same night. He nodded back at Paul with the same slight smile, opened the concealed door, took one last look at the morning's destruction, and then exited to attend to his assigned task.

MISSY

Paul watched Luc as he headed out the door, and fleetingly remembered the night the two of them became "brothers." The look in his eyes was the same look he had back then... dismay, unbelief. He knew Luc didn't understand everything that was going on, but the truth was... neither did he. It was a unique bond they had, this unspoken unity of spirit, and the existence of such always gave Paul a deep sense of peace.

As Luc disappeared, he turned his attention to his little sister. "C'mon, sis. I'll take you home."

Missy's face lit up with anticipation. This wasn't something Paul offered very often, and she was not about to lose the chance to have some fun. "On your bike? Can I wear your helmet?"

"Sure," he said in a fun, father-like voice, but quickly betrayed some lingering concerns, "you know what's off limits, though."

Turning with immediacy toward his cycle, she grabbed the helmet and put it on, then sheepishly responded to her older brother's warning. "Now, Paul... do I ever fool with those commands?"

"Well, let me think. I *do* remember getting a ticket once... for going 123," he reminded her.

"I remember *peeing* in my pants," she quickly rebounded. "How was I supposed to know what 'escape' meant. Besides, you didn't *have* to pull over for that cop. "

They both had a good laugh at this, and then boarded the

37

motorcycle. As he settled in, his stomach reminded him with a growl that it needed food.

"You hungry, babe?"

"As a horse!"

"Okay... whenever you're ready."

"On," she said, and the visor slid down as the motor came to life. With a spin of the back wheel, gravel and dust spitting behind them, they sped down the winding road away from the warehouses and headed to their favorite little place to eat.

Missy clung tight to her older brother, once again grateful that he was alive and in one piece. More often than not these days she was battling the panic that came with each new phone call. Would this call be the one that dropped the hammer on her heart? Or maybe the next one carried with it the news that Paul was dead. Memories kept flooding her mind as they cruised the highway: Paul and Tony wrestling in the back seat of the old Dodge Caravan, her parents singing those old Christian rock songs that always drove her nuts. It wasn't that she didn't like the songs, because the truth was she loved them. But maybe Mom and Dad could get some singing lessons. Then Tony would pop his head up from behind the back seat and start drenching her with his powered water pistol, Paul lurking in the wait with some reinforcements. There were so many good memories of the family, and of how Paul, Tony and she always found a way to have the best of times. How she longed so deeply for those days to return, and she found herself holding back tears as they cruised the highway.

Paul decided to listen to some more of the CD while they headed toward breakfast. He'd liked the first song he listened to, although he wasn't quite sure what to make of the lyrics...

There comes a time
in everyone's life,
When you've got to face the answers
to the questions of your heart.

You come to a fork
in the middle of the road,
and you've got to make a choice
of which path you'll travel on.

> *Give me direction, give me some hope.*
> *Give me your love and a hand to hold.*
> *Give me a purpose, give me a dream.*
> *Give me your life, and set me free.*

Paul turned the music off as they approached the diner their parents used to bring them to every Sunday after church. Going there was still sort of a ritual for the two of them.

It was a typical diner—cinderblock construction, flat roof with vents for the exhaust hood, a couple of awnings, a glass door with stickers showing what credit cards they accepted. Inside, the tables were simple and solid, nothing but booth seating. The checkered linoleum floor was clean, but would obviously never take wax again. Each table had two napkins on it, silverware that didn't quite match, and two coffee cups turned upside down on their saucers. It had a familiar smell of smoked meats and sweet maple, indicating it was indeed breakfast time.

Paul and Missy entered the diner, which had a decent crowd, but nowhere near capacity. It only had one person working the floor, doing both the seating and the waiting. They stood at a sign that read, "Please wait to be seated," and Paul took advantage of the time to be the big brother he was.

"You guys are pretty hot these days... you and Mark."

Missy's hand unconsciously and gently went to her stomach. "Oh, I don't know about that."

Paul feigned irritation, "What do you mean you don't know? You're hardly ever apart!" In a mock sarcastic tone, arms open wide for emphasis, he continued, "I don't know."

Two can play this game, she thought, and then, acting hurt, replied, "Gosh, Paul..."

Paul smiled at her. "Hey, sis, I'm just kidding."

She smiled back at him. "I know... me too."

He grabbed her and began rubbing his knuckles in her hair, to her chagrin.

"Stop it! Stop it!"

He stopped as the waitress finally made her way up to them. "Good morning," she said. "Table for two?"

"Three. Me, her," Paul said, acknowledging he and Missy, then pointing to an empty space next to them, "and him."

The waitress chuckled politely, and took the "three" of them to an empty booth by the front window. She passed out three menus as they were seated, getting into the humor of the moment.

"The usual?" Paul asked Missy.

"Fine with me."

"We'll both have the chocolate chip pancakes with whipped cream, and some chocolate milk," he told the waitress.

"Mmmmm... sounds... rich," she said, smiling. "Anything else?"

Paul turned to the empty seat next to him, and conversed with the third member of their party. "What d'ya want?" Turning back to the waitress, he responded, "Coffee and a twinkie for him."

"Now stop that," the waitress said in mock anger. She waved him off and went to turn in their order, laughing all the way to the kitchen. *She obviously needs to get out more,* Paul thought, as he and Missy watched her walk away.

They sat there in awkward silence, and it was clear that something was on Missy's mind. Paul broke the silence first.

"How far along are you?"

She looked at him funny, taken aback and flushed with guilt at the same time.

"You touched your stomach when I mentioned you and Mark," he continued.

Missy paused for a minute or so, unable to make eye contact with her big brother. Finally, with a resolved look, she answered, "About two months. I've known for a couple of weeks, though."

"Does Mark know?"

She looked out the window to the parking lot that was in front and stared at Paul's motorcycle, not able to say anything.

"He is the father, right?"

That brought her back quickly. "Of course he is. Who else would it be?"

"Well, you didn't say anything," he replied.

Again, there was a heavy pause. "I might not tell him."

"Why not?"

"He doesn't have to know."

"He's the father, for Christ's sake!" Paul said, a little too loudly.

She looked away from him again for a moment, and then replied very tentatively, "I'm not sure I'm going have it."

Paul perked up and looked deep into her eyes.

"I'm scared, Paul," she continued. "Look at the world today.

Look at Tony, *our own blood,* killing all those innocent people. I'm not so sure it would be the right thing to do."

Paul became very emphatic. "So, because of Tony, you shouldn't have the kid? Sorry, babe, but I don't see the connection."

Missy continued, "It's not *just* Tony. It's him, you, Luc, Billy… all of you. With so much hatred, well… what's happening… to *all* of us? We used to love each other, hang out together. Good or bad, we always stood by each other. Now you guys spend more energy trying to hurt each other…"

There was a long pause, as her words seemed to hang in the air.

"I don't know, babe," Paul said evenly.

"Do you still love him?" she asked.

"Tony?" He knew whom she was referring to. She nodded anyway. "Yes… I think. I don't want to hurt him; he just has to be stopped."

This made Missy very upset. "By *you?*"

"Maybe," he replied honestly. "It sure looks like it right now."

She quietly pleaded with him, "Just, please, please don't *become* him." She paused before continuing, "I can see it happening, Paul."

"Oh, please," he said sarcastically. "We are two very different people."

"Are you sure of that?" she asked rhetorically.

They sat in silence again, both looking down at the table, playing uncomfortably with the silverware. Paul knew, deep down, that she had legitimate reason to be concerned. Clearly, his frustration with the ambivalence of Billy and the authorities toward the increased violence was becoming evident in his impatience with those around him. He certainly was nothing like Tony; but it seemed the thing he was striving against was beginning to influence him negatively. Missy was right in many respects. All the pain and hatred that surrounded life itself was gaining victory in everyone's heart. *Why even fight it anymore,* he thought. *Nothing's changed, and things are getting worse.* All he could do was brew in these kinds of thoughts.

The air was getting thicker with each agonizing moment, when, finally, the waitress arrived at the table with their pancakes and milks. She also gave "Dan" the coffee and twinkie "he" ordered.

"What's that?" Paul asked her.

"His coffee and twinkie."

Paul looked at Missy, then back to the waitress. "His, who? You okay? You want to sit down… take a break, maybe?"

The waitress fleetingly considered the idea, and then walked away, shaking her head and laughing out loud as she did.

Once they had some privacy again, Paul gently reached across the table, took Missy's hand in his own, and looked deep into her eyes. "Listen… I love you, very much. I only want what's best for you… and I'll always be there when you need me."

Missy squeezed his hand hard. "I know, but I'm afraid. I don't know what to do."

"Well, you have to tell Mark," Paul said, "about the baby. You're both part of that child, and *it* is part of both of you. He should be part of the decision."

"I know," she said, with a considerable sigh, "you're right… *as always.*"

That last part was just a bit sarcastic, he thought to himself. Paul made her look in his eyes. "And about me becoming Tony… it'll never happen. I don't think I could ever have that much hate inside me. I just wish I could understand why he does what he does."

Missy's grip became gentler. "All I'm saying is be careful. He seems to get worse every day, more… evil."

"Okay, okay, I'll be careful," he said, trying to laugh off both her and the subject.

"I'm serious, Paul," she said flatly.

"I'll be careful, I promise," he reassured her. "Now, let's dig in."

The pancakes didn't stand a chance. Their physical and nervous hunger taking control, both ate with vigor, few words being exchanged. They finished off the meal in short order, and then hit the road once again.

A million unconnected thoughts ran through Paul's mind as he took Missy home, and he finished listening to the rest of that song he started on the way to the diner…

> *Broad is the path,*
> *And wide is the gate.*
> *Destruction waits for those*
> *Who follow that way.*
>
> *Straight is the path,*
> *And narrow is the gate,*
> *Life is for those*
> *Who choose to follow the way.*
>
> *Give me direction, give me your hope.*
> *Give me the strength, to travel this road.*
> *Give me a purpose, give me your dream.*
> *Give me your light, guide my destiny.*

For Missy, the excitement of the ride there was in the past. As they pulled into the driveway, she got off the bike and gave Paul back the revered helmet.

"Thanks for breakfast. I'm stuffed."

"Anytime, sis," Paul said with a wink, as he put the helmet on.

She stared at the ground for a bit, and then spoke timidly without looking him in the eyes. "I just don't know what to do, Paul."

Tenderly lifting his sister's chin, Paul spoke the only advice he knew to give at this point. "Just follow your heart, sis. Everything will work out." He made some final adjustments to his helmet, for comfort, and revved his motorcycle, more to calm his nerves than anything else. "Keep smiling, okay?"

She kissed her hand and then touched his face through the visor-hole. "I love you, big brother."

"I love you too, babe." He looked at his watch, already fidgety from wanting to get going. "Gotta go. I'll see you later."

The visor closed and Paul immediately set off. Missy stood and watched him until he was no longer in view, then went in the house.

THE GANG

Cruising up the road toward the warehouse, Paul was pleased to see from the cars parked around it that Mark had succeeded in getting everyone to the meeting—John, Tommy, Pete, Nathan, Luc, Tim, Mark, Phil, Jim, Matt, and Joey. Mark was young, and didn't always understand why he was being asked to do what Paul often requested. But, he was diligent and enthusiastic. Paul would have no qualms, whatsoever, about having him as part of his family. That is, if Missy chose to have it that way.

He pulled up next to the main entrance to his warehouse, turned off his motorcycle, and made his way through the damage toward the hidden door. He could hear the friendly male banter going on as he headed down the stairs, along with the high-pitched giggles from some of the guys' girlfriends. Paul wasn't too comfortable with the inclusion of the women, but they always seemed to have a perspective that kept things in balance.

As he entered the room, he saw Luc sitting at the desk, coolly watching as the rest of the group exchanged barbs. He seldom entered into these verbal jousting matches, but that made sense. He was the silent, calculating one of the group. Next to him was Pete, leaning against the wall in a tilted chair. The "old man," as the rest of the group called him, he was easily fifteen to twenty years senior to most of them. With his long salt-and-pepper hair and close-cropped beard, he certainly looked the part of the old man.

Surveying the group very quickly, Paul wondered how it was that so many of them were so young. Excluding Luc, Pete, and himself, none of them were older than their early twenties. Their age was a challenge for Paul. They lacked experience and often acted out of zeal, unchecked by the wisdom garnered from those very years of life they lacked. But, it also served to Paul's advantage, as they usually afforded him and Pete the honor and respect that their age deserved... a quality rare and difficult to find these days. He looked at Mark, sitting all the way across the room, laughing boisterously, wondering what his reaction was going to be when Missy told him about their baby. It was strange knowing this, and Mark not, like they were playing cards and he knew the hand Mark was dealt.

"Yo, Joey," Phil said, pointing to the shot-up warehouse upstairs. "That place looks like your bedroom."

"What? I cleaned it yesterday," Joey replied. "Ain't that right, Johnny-boy?"

"Yeah," John confirmed. "But we stopped excavating when we hit oil, though."

"Ahhh," said Joey, waving him off, "we found your panties, too."

John was unperturbed by the friendly jab at his manhood. "The red ones or the black ones?"

"The *pink* ones," Phil exclaimed, making the whole group laugh.

Like most conversations of the kind, the subject quickly changed. "Anyone know who won the Laker game last night?" Matt asked.

"Miami spanked them good," said one of the girls, a beautiful red-head, "by eighteen."

The guys were impressed that she knew this. "Bummer! I had fifty bucks on 'em," Matt admitted sadly.

"A fool and his money," Jim said in a teacherly tone. "Face it, Matt. The Lakers suck."

Matt pointed his finger like a gun at him in a mock threat. "Watch your mouth... I've killed for less than that."

"All they need is a new coach," the girl said.

Another guy, Tommy, didn't like the sound of that. "Get rid of Magic? You're out of your mind."

"He was a great player, sure... but he just simply can't coach," the girl retorted.

Paul listened to it all, gauging the mood of the group. He never ceased to be amazed at the vibrancy of attitude that existed amongst these guys. All of them, in one way or another, had suffered through terrible losses—family members killed, businesses destroyed, homes obliterated. Some of them were deeply religious, while others didn't have a clue what it was they believed in. But they all had one thing in common: they hated what was happening to their town and their world. It wasn't unique, what was happening there. All over the world, anarchy was the rule of the land.

Everything had started to come apart back at the turn of the century, shortly after the terrorist attacks on the Twin Towers in New York. The US went on the offensive, going into the Middle East in her "war against terror." It was difficult, and the world was divided over what was taking place. Paul, for his own part, was very supportive of what his government was doing. After all, the US had been attacked by an isolated bunch of extremist fanatics, driven by hatred of a nation that supported their greatest enemy. At least, that was how it appeared back then.

Turns out they weren't so isolated, because after many years of spot-wars throughout that region, the true nature of the real war became more evident.

Nation upon nation that had been allied with the US began to betray their "friend" to reveal their true motives. Driven by hatred, yes, but the real enemy wasn't the United States. Religion was at the core of what drove those people, and the terrorism soon spread beyond national identities. Those "extremists" turned out to be the front-line of a very deep and far-reaching agenda.

Like a flashlight directly in one's eyes, Paul was shaken from his thoughts with a question.

"What do you think, Paul?" the girl asked.

"About what?" Paul replied, acting like he didn't know what they were talking about.

Matt laughed, and filled Paul in. "She thinks the Lakers should can Magic."

"You're nuts!" Paul said, simply.

"That's what I said," Tommy agreed.

The girl rolled her eyes and threw up her arms in surrender as she sat down. "You guys are hopeless!"

Paul took that as his cue to get down to the task at hand. Taking a deep breath, he quickly brought their focus to the one thing on his mind: to figure out how to stop this insanity at home.

"All right, everybody, listen up. We don't have much time. As you could see by the condition of the place, there was a bit of a problem here this morning. Some of Tony's—"

He cut himself off as he saw that someone was missing. "Hey, where's Tim? I saw his car parked out front."

There was the sound of a flushing toilet behind Mark, and a door opening hastily.

"I'm coming," Tim said, entering the room exasperated. "Jesus, can't a man relieve himself with dignity anymore?"

"Prunes do not a dignified man make," said Phil in a philosophical, Shakespearean voice. Everyone in the room laughed, and Tim replied in kind.

"Prune this!" he said as he flipped up the one-finger salute.

Paul laughed hard at that, but then quickly got everyone back on track. "Okay, okay. Let's get started. As I was saying, a couple of Tony's dweebs had a wake-up call for me this morning."

"They're getting pretty bold these days," Tommy said.

"They're all crazy!" said Jim.

"Possessed is more like it," Tommy replied.

"Regardless, we've gotta figure them out. I was telling Luc earlier," Paul continued, "they're always a step ahead of us. And the cops, well, I don't think they care one bit, because nothing ever gets done."

One guy who had sat silently throughout was Nathan, which fit his demeanor very well. "You can say that again," he piped up.

"They own the cops, man. It's so obvious they look the other way," said Joey.

Paul corrected him. "Not everyone, Joey."

Joey bit back. "C'mon, Paul, open your eyes. Don't let your friendship with Billy blind you."

"I grew up with the guy!" Paul exclaimed defensively.

Tommy jumped in to defend Joey. "Billy's a wuss. He won't make a move at all. There's plenty of evidence pointing at Tony. *Obvious* stuff."

Luc had finally heard enough of this back-and-forth. He'd been doing the research, and could clearly see a trend that made his insides churn. He found himself thinking back to all the times that his family would have discussions about how the world would gradually spin out of control until the Lord would finally return. He wondered if this was what was beginning to happen.

His voice was loud with frustration and contention. "Obvious, yeah, but does it matter? I'm tellin' ya, this goes much deeper than the cops. There's always a judge or politician to step in and argue some constitutional or civil rights point."

The tension in the room was growing rapidly, the friction between everyone making the room hot.

Nathan sat forward in his chair, arguing his point. "He could at least try… he could still do something."

"Not if his hands are tied," Luc countered.

Paul was a bit surprised by Luc's outburst. Seldom did he ever jump into the fray like this. "Enough already," he said sternly. "Let's not fight each other. Let's be constructive here. We all want to stop Tony, especially *me*. But… let's do it right. Don't forget, the police haven't stopped *us* either."

Nathan laughed sarcastically, then replied, "What's there to stop, Paul? What have we done?"

Paul stared at Nathan, ready to defend the actions of their group. But then, realizing he was right, looked away in defeat and turned to Luc. "What did you find out, Luc?"

Luc was prepared for this. "Well, in the past six months, it looks like Tony's been focusing on young people." He pulled up some statistics on the com-link screen, and continued. "Let's see… an elementary school and high school, two school buses and a day-care center. They've also hit a library, a synagogue, and numerous small businesses. All totaled, about 900 dead, 2100 injured; 70% of these were 16 or younger. The only other line I could find was, except for the library, there's always a religious affiliation involved. They hadn't made a hit in three weeks, until this morning."

"This morning was just a warning of sorts, though" Paul said in response.

Phil spoke up with highly charged youthful exuberance, "We ought to just break loose right now—"

"Yeah, an eye for an eye," Joey concurred.

Tim countered, "And lower ourselves to their level? *We're* not the scum—they are."

"And they aren't afraid at all," said Jim. "Maybe if they had a price to pay for their actions, they'd think twice before acting."

Mark finally spoke up. He had tried to remain silent, but gave in to the tension building in the room.

"Or maybe they would act with more fire," he said in a condescending tone.

Nathan stood up and began an angry discourse on how he felt about things. "What are we afraid of? Did you hear Luc? They just keep comin'. It doesn't matter *what* we do. I'm tired of tip-toeing around. My little brother is dead because of them, and I want blood."

Mark had very little patience for this kind of self-pity, and leaned forward in his seat to emphasize this. Pointing his finger in Nathan's direction, he expressed his distaste.

"Like you're the only one who's lost family to this hell? Look around you, man. You're not alone. Stop feeling sorry for yourself—"

The rebuttal was cut off mid-sentence by Nathan's own response, a hurtling fist that found its target squarely on Mark's jaw. Before Mark could realize what had happened and respond, several in the room had already gotten between them, the girls backing away.

Paul was pounding the table like a judge in an unruly courtroom. "Stop it, all of you!"

Nathan now turned on Paul, fist raised behind his head and still full of anger and adrenaline. "You stop it!"

With the speed of a feud-tested gunslinger, Paul whipped his Magnum from its holster, clicked back its hammer and held it point blank in front of Nathan's face—stopping him dead in his tracks and silencing the room immediately. Staring straight down the barrel of his gun, into the wide open, panic-stricken eyes of his young friend, he held his position long enough for Nathan's rage to fade.

The look in Paul's eyes was one that Nathan had seen before, and he, for one, didn't want to be at the receiving end of the usual response. Paul was his friend, his mentor, and the last thing he wanted was to lose his trust and respect. Besides, he knew Paul well enough, and didn't want to die just yet.

With just as much speed and accuracy as he exhibited on readying his gun, Paul twirled the Magnum on his finger like a seasoned western showman, and holstered the weapon.

He then spoke in a deliberate and even tone. "Please, sit down everyone."

Everyone took their seats submissively, but Nathan continued to stand in defiance, trying to save some morsel of pride. The last one, he finally sat down in his own chair, sullen and ashamed. With his chin to his chest, he rolled his eyes up to look at Paul, who was returning the gaze with that of a father who might be glad to see a child return home after a defiant night away; eyes saddened, but with a slight smile that revealed relief... and the chance to breathe once again.

"We've *all* lost family and friends, each and every one of us," Paul said to the group. "We've come together now to try to stop this craziness—"

Mark cut him off, his eyes closed, rubbing his chin because the pain of the punch hadn't quite reached its fullness yet. "They're all freakin' psycho, man!"

Paul started to reply, "Maybe so—"

Joey stood up, continuing Mark's thought. "And they get worse every time. It's like they enjoy it... like they get off on it, man. We should just kill them all right now."

Paul tried to reason with him, suppressing his own anger at the group's sudden contentiousness. "If we did what you say, we'd be just like them."

Joey was obviously not pleased with this response, and would have none of it. "They *deserve* to die."

Paul again tried to reason, recalling what Steve had said to him earlier in the day. "Killing... is killing." He found himself struggling, as well, with the words of his own sister. "Are we really any different than Tony?"

Like a hand-grenade that exploded in their midst, the entire group suddenly turned on him, all at once. Initially he found himself feeling defensive, but, instead, found some humor in this outburst; at least now they were all of one accord again. He let the murmur of the group settle a bit, then answered his own question.

"Not if we kill intentionally. *Saving* lives is what this is all about, what we're fighting for. If anyone disagrees with that, then there's the door."

The group fell silent as they all looked around the room,

shrugging shoulders, nodding and shaking their heads. It appeared that order had finally been restored, when Joey stood up abruptly, his face flushed red with obvious disgust.

"You guys are pathetic," he yelled at the group, then pointed at Paul. "And you... you never stand up to your brother. I'm sick of this, and sick of you. You may not do anything, but I will. I'm outta here." He spun around, looking at each person in the group. "Anyone else?"

He waited for a moment, expecting at least Nathan to leap to his side, but no one else got up to join him. He turned to leave, and as he did he grabbed his girlfriend's hand, assuming she would go with him. However, she pulled her hand back from his, looking away from him in disdain. He stopped in amazement, staring at her in the uncomfortable silence of the group, then left, swearing all the way out the door and up the stairs. John eventually got up to follow. Just before departing, he took a quick glance at Paul, with the look of regret filling his eyes. His own loyalty had to be with his brother.

No longer able to hide his frustration, pounding the table with his fists as the door upstairs closed, Paul sang his own profane song beneath his breath. Turning on his heels, his back to the group, he gathered himself with four deep breaths. After regaining his composure, he slowly turned back to Luc. "You got anything else?"

"Nothing concrete," he answered with a sigh. "It seems like this could be some kind of persecution or inquisition, though, if you look at the pattern and how it's carried out. You know how things are anymore."

Paul pounded the table in resolve. "Well, let's find out, for Christ's sake. Any suggestions?"

Pete responded immediately with conviction. "First of all, let's stick together. We've got to look out for each other if we're going to make it work and stay alive."

Why had it taken so long for him to speak up? That wasn't like him, at all. Paul resisted the temptation to say a word or two about stating the obvious, refraining from doing so out of respect for the old man, and for their friendship. Instead he addressed the group.

"I can agree to that. The rest of you?"

The group agreed emphatically in a chorus of nods and "yeahs."

"What else?"

Pete offered an idea. "Maybe we could start tailing those guys, like they do us. Find out what they're doing and what they're up to."

Paul was unsure. "I don't know—"

"Come on, Paul," Pete continued, "some of what Joey said was right. We *should* be doing more. They tail us. Why not turn the table?"

Now Paul understood Pete's silence earlier. He, too, felt a sense of helplessness in the face of all this. He was also feeling frustrated, but wasn't about to disrespect Paul in front of the younger guys. Still, one thing was becoming crystal clear, and that was that everyone was beginning to feel as if they were serving no real purpose in all of this. *Maybe Steve is right,* Paul thought. *Maybe none of this matters anymore.*

"Easier said than done," was Nathan's response, snapping Paul back to the present.

Joey's now ex-girlfriend offered, "Not if we help, and some family and friends help out, too."

Mark agreed. "Yeah, I'm sure they would, and if anything looks suspicious we could check into it."

The group collectively nodded and affirmed its agreement.

Paul was still very unsure about this new course of action. But, fully understanding that things could not continue as they currently were, he surrendered in agreement. "Okay, but one of *us* has to be with them at all times."

"No problem," Pete said. "Everyone check in with me and we'll get this organized."

"I'll keep digging up info, maybe squeeze some stuff from Billy," Luc offered.

"We could start taggin' those guys starting today," Jim said confidently.

Paul cautioned him, "Okay, but be careful. Use your head and stay out of sight."

Paul cringed again at another statement of the obvious, not liking what was going on but realizing it needed to be done, if only for the sanity of the group.

"Heyyy," Jim responded, doing a really bad "Fonzie" imitation, thumbs-up and all.

Paul smiled at that, and addressed the group one last time before they began to file out. "All right, people. Let's do it! Stay positive, be careful, and stay in touch with each other."

Everyone got up to leave, talking amongst themselves. Nathan was quick to catch up to Mark, who was opening and closing his mouth, as if that would cause the pain from the earlier punch to disappear. "Hey, Mark." Mark looked over at him, giving thought to decking him then and there. "Man, I'm really sorry about what happened."

Mark forgot the pain for a second, and remembered the

depth of camaraderie they all shared. "It's okay," he said rubbing his jaw. "I got an extra. Besides, it didn't hurt." He was lying, and they both knew it.

As they headed up the stairs together, Nathan continued, "But I was wrong, totally wrong."

Mark draped his arm around Nathan's shoulders, forgiving and smiling. "No problem, dude." Squeezing Nathan's head between his arm and chest, he added, "Next time… I'll rip your heart out." They both laughed heartily. "Hey, you hungry?"

"Sure am," Nathan replied.

"Great," Mark exclaimed victoriously, "your treat."

They were the last two to exit the room.

PLANS

Paul, Luc, and Pete were the only ones left in the warehouse. All three were weary from the tension of the meeting. Pete broke the silence.

"I hear Steve's back in town," he said to Paul.

"I guess so," Paul replied evasively.

Pete looked at him expectantly. "Well?"

Paul hesitated to answer. The last thing he wanted right now was to talk about Steve, and Pete's inquiry was beginning to irritate him. "Well, what? Steve is back. I don't like it, but there's nothing I can do about it."

Luc tried reasoning with him. "You can't hate him forever, Paul."

This entire day was beginning to wear thin on Paul, and his irritation at this particular conversation was making him defensive.

"I don't *hate* him. I just think he did the wrong thing, and coming back won't change that."

"I agree," Pete said, trying to be diplomatic, "but you gotta let the past be the past. Press on, man. It'll kill you if you don't."

"Yeah, right," Paul retorted, adding sarcasm to the emotions already on his sleeve.

Luc decided to try and change the subject completely. "Hey, look… what do you say we all go out tonight?"

"Sorry, I can't," Pete answered.

"That's all we ever hear from you anymore, man," said Luc.

Pete took a turn at being defensive. "Hey, I'm busy. Maybe next time, okay?"

Paul jumped in. "You know what I think, Luc. Some chick's got him whipped, bad."

"Yeah," Luc agreed, "he has been kind of mellowed-out lately."

"So what? We're not getting any younger. Are we, Paul?" Pete shot back.

Paul laughed. "Gimme a break, Pete. I haven't gotten past adolescence."

"Let's go sow some oats, then," Luc volunteered, ready to go somewhere, anywhere. "How 'bout the old standby?"

"Emphasis on *old*," laughed Pete.

"I don't know," Paul deadpanned.

"C'mon, Paul," Luc pleaded. "Loosen up. It'll be fun. Hey, you may even get laid, bro. How long's it been?"

Paul thought for a moment, trying desperately to think of a come-back to Luc's friendly attack on his manly prowess. "Last night… your sister." Immediately Paul regretted what he said, remembering how Luc lost his family.

But Luc, being the laid-back kind of guy he was, took it all in stride. He laughed out loud, and the other two joined him in reveling in such middle-school humor. "What do ya say?" Luc pleaded one last time.

Paul thought it over for a moment, and then smiled. "Why not? What time?"

"How's ten sound?"

"Nine-thirty? We can grab a bite to eat, first."

Luc was pleased. "You got it. Nine-thirty it is. Later, dude!"

"Later," Paul said.

"See ya, Paul," Pete said, flashing him a peace sign with his fingers.

"Yeah, peace, dude. Call me when you get this stuff together, okay?"

"Will do."

As Pete and Luc left, Paul found himself alone in the room, and allowed himself to fall into the seat at the desk. With everything that had occurred so far, thanks to Pete he found himself thinking only of Steve. There was a time when it would have been the *four* of them talking after a meeting like this morning's, with Steve often leading the conversation. Instead, he was now struggling with a sense of betrayal again. He had almost let all of that go, but now it was like a hundred-pound backpack weighing him down. *I really should have stayed in bed,* he thought to himself again.

"Why, Steve?" Paul thought aloud. "Why'd you come back?"

THE GAME

Dry afternoon heat radiated from the asphalt parking lot, which served an ordinary, but fairly good-sized, two-story building of brick and stucco. The sign identifying the establishment was an exact duplicate of the picture on the CD Steve had given to Paul that morning—mountains, road, storm and sunrise…

Damascus Road
The end… and a new beginning

It seemed a bit out of place standing atop the roof, in stark contrast to the drab gray and earthy colors of the main building, but that contrast seemed a perfect metaphor for Steve, who was, himself, a contrast between the old and the new.

Inside it looked like a typical club with lots of seating and padded booths dressed in chocolate brown, faux leather. To the right of the double glass doors, as one walked in, was a long bar that ran the length of the wall, padded in that same faux leather, with a brass foot rail about a foot off the floor. This coordinated well with the brass-legged, padded bar stools.

None of it was fancy, which succeeded in drawing your attention to the one non-typical element of the club—two huge, dark pink granite tablets above the bar area, occupying a good fifty percent of the wall space, with a listing of The Ten Commandments etched into the stone in black lettering. This was Steve's pride and joy, and brought him the most satisfaction.

Directly across from the bar, some 100 feet away on the other side of the floor, was the focal point of the club—a sort of half-circle stage that offered ample room for the patrons to gather around and watch whatever band was playing. The second-floor level wrapped around the stage like a glove, and gave the aura of a small theater. One thing was certain: nobody in the place would have a bad view.

A top-notch sound and light system ruled the roost, consisting of two stacks of amps, for the guitar and bass, respectively, four floor monitors, and four five-foot tall stacks of speakers for the house. Across the ceiling above the stage were sixteen light cans that allowed for the coolest light spectacles. All of this was run by one huge, computerized mixing board that handled both jobs simultaneously, in coordination with each other, nestled in an enclosed booth halfway between the bar and the stage. This system would make any sound or light engineer salivate, and it was easy to see how bands might find it impossible to keep their music confined to the building. That suited Steve just fine.

Inside the building, prepping the place for that night's business, Steve saw the police car drive by and then double back. The club wasn't scheduled to open for hours still, and the lot was empty. He figured he knew who was driving by because this was becoming sort of a daily ritual, so he stepped outside to wait. Maybe this time he'd stop in. Leaning up against the building, arms folded, right foot on the wall and left leg acting as anchor, his body language spoke of confidence and self-assurance.

The police car came into the parking lot this time and pulled right up to where Steve was standing, a little closer than the average person might feel comfortable with. A familiar figure stepped out of the driver's side, slowly and deliberately, and stood just inside the open car door, looking over the top at Steve on the passenger side. The attitude was light, but had an air of confrontation that could be sensed right away. A contemptuous, yellow grin came across his face as he addressed Steve.

"I never knew you were a *businessman*," Billy said in an overdone sarcastic drawl.

Steve glanced back at the building, then said evenly, "God has ways of changing men, y'know."

Billy cared little for Steve's God, or anything He had to do involving Steve. He just wanted some answers. "Why'd you come back, Steve?" he demanded.

"Business," Steve replied with a subtle shrug of his shoulders, turning his eyes toward Billy again.

Billy chuckled in sarcasm, answering, "A rock bar?"

"Let's just say I'm doing some fishing," Steve mimicked in an exaggerated drawl, with the intent to irritate.

Billy, succumbing to the bait, blurted impatiently, "Jesus Christ… we know what you're doin'—"

Steve, sensing he had the upper ground in this debate, cut him off. "And Jesus knows exactly what *you're* doing. I've always suspected you, Billy; you, and Tony, and everything that's going on around here."

Billy nearly swallowed his Skoal at the direct accusation just made, and struggled to control the anger that was turning his face beet red. "You got no idea what's goin' on 'round here. You ain't got all the answers, and believe it or not… your light don't shine at all around here, not in my book anyway."

"It's not *my* light I'm pointing to, and it's not *your* book I read."

"You're asking for trouble, boy. This kind of light," he pointed to the building, "gets put out these days."

"The light always shines, but you're just too blind to see it," Steve said, smirking. "Y'know the sad thing about all this, Billy? It's that you're just an insignificant little pawn in this game… and you don't even realize it."

Billy had had enough of this, and thought it best to back off—for now.

"The train is bearing down on you, Steve. Best know when to get off the track… *boy*." He got into his car and started it.

Steve bent over, leaned on the passenger side door, and spoke with unbridled confidence.

"Checkmate, Billy." The strange look of confusion on Billy's face said wonders.

"My King has already won," he continued, stepping away from the cruiser.

Billy revved up the car emphatically, saluting Steve with the "bird," and then peeled out of the lot, fishtailing all the way, leaving a trail of rubber several yards long.

THE GYM

It's time to unload some of the burden, Paul thought, as he wove his motorcycle with reckless abandon through the traffic. Someone was going to bare the brunt of the day's turbulent maelstrom, and his victim was waiting for him in the building just ahead.

He pulled into the parking lot with a little too much bravado, and skidded into a parking spot just outside the main entrance. Forgetting to remove his helmet, or secure his "motor," he bound toward the entrance, leaping over the three steps leading to the front door with anticipation oozing from every pore. Suddenly remembering his gear on the bike, he made a quick U-turn, sprinted back to his cycle, grabbed the bag that was bungeed to the back of the seat, and turned once again for the entrance to the building.

"Off, Alarm," he commanded.

As he reached for the front door and opened it to go inside, an explosion of sound filled the air around him, and his head snapped backward. For a split second he lost awareness of everything around him. His body tensed up, and prepared itself to fight to the end for survival. Just as quickly, Paul realized he was still holding the door in his hand. He hit his head with the door as he opened it, and his helmet insulated him from the impact. Chuckling to himself, he moved inside the building, and continued toward his objective.

He took little notice of the nice-looking girls that asked for his membership card at the front desk, swiped it through the reader, and handed it back to him with a clean, warm towel. To his left, behind the entry counter, was a doorway leading to the aquatics area. In his focused state, though, he didn't give the lifeguards in their scant red bikinis a second look. Moving through the door to his right, he entered the main area with determination. *He's going down today,* Paul thought to himself, his pace quickening. *He's going down.*

The lobby area was a good fifty feet long by twenty feet wide, with the aerobics room to the left, running it's full length and separated by a full-height glass wall. About a dozen people were just meandering about, some watching the class taking place in the aerobics room, and others retrieving some sort of healthy juice or snack from the vending machines that lined the other walls. Some two-thirds of the way down the right side of the lobby was a doorway leading to the gym, and this was Paul's objective. Removing his helmet as he made his way through the lobby, he glanced toward the aerobics class.

That's when he saw her—blond, petite, blue eyes, in her early to mid-20's. Everything around him moved in slow motion, and just like in the movies, the world around her disappeared into a fog. She was heavily involved in the class, and her rhythmic movements to the music were hypnotic to him. He didn't realize he was still walking until he ran into the door frame at the entrance to the gym, dropping his helmet as he did.

Once again, he was jolted back to the here-and-now, and quickly reached down to pick up his helmet. He then stopped for a moment to regroup. The sound of bouncing basketballs and clanging exercise and weight machines reminded him of his original obsession. Stepping into the gym, he took a quick look over his shoulder into the aerobics room, hoping for one more glimpse of beauty perfected.

In the middle of the gym was a ¾-size basketball court, with a 4-lane track that encircled it. On both sides of the building, to the outside of the 1/10th-mile track, were dozens of hydraulic weight machines filled with people, young and old, vigorously pushing their bodies to the limit.

Coach saw Paul's "grand" entrance and laughed, waving to him as he approached. He was leading an exercise class on the machines, and told them to take five with his hand and fingers stretched out, then made his way toward Paul. Their handshake was sincere as they met in the middle of the track, to the left of the basketball court.

"Nice entrance, Grace," Coach teased with a huge smile on his face. "All those ballet classes paying off, I see."

"Whatever," was the only response Paul could think of.

"Where you been?" Coach asked. "Haven't seen you around much, lately."

"You know how it is, Coach. Things come up," Paul replied, admiring for the umpteenth time how fit and lean Coach was for a man in his mid-40's.

"And out," Coach said, patting Paul's belly, calipers in hand. "You have to let me put 'Jaws' on you before you go," he said, holding them up to Paul's head.

Batting the calipers away as if swatting a pesky fly, Paul shared a spontaneous laugh with his exercise mentor. "You'd love that, wouldn't you? Then you could justify calling me a fathead."

"What goes around comes around," Coach rebuked, good-naturedly. "Remember when I first started?"

"*Please,*" Paul pleaded. "Don't kick me when I'm down. Besides," he paused for dramatic impact, "you *were* fat."

Coach waved his hand in front of Paul's face, Three Stooges-style, and in his best Curly voice replied, "Oh… wise guy, eh?"

Paul looked at the clock above the row of exercise machines, realizing he was wasting time and keeping his victim waiting far too long. "Hey, I gotta change," he said. "Chip and I are running full court."

"Yeah, I know," Coach said. "He's psyched for you."

His victim, on the court near the basket by the gym entrance, was staring over at Paul and covering his face with his hand, pointing at him mockingly and smiling.

"I can see that, Coach."

"He was burning everyone yesterday, especially from the top," Coach warned.

Paul began to wonder just who the victim was actually going to be. "Thanks for the encouragement, Coach. You're a big help."

"What are friends for? Don't forget to stretch first."

"Armstrong I am," he replied, turning to head for the locker. But the blonde girl from the aerobics class immediately overcame his thoughts, so he took a deliberate detour back out the entrance, and walked over to the aerobics room. He stopped in his tracks as he caught sight of her again. The instructor, used to having guys stop and watch the class, smiled and waved at him, but he didn't notice. He was transfixed, completely mesmerized, by the aura of absolute beauty this woman possessed. It wasn't until she saw him looking at her, via the mirror in the room, that he snapped out of his trance. Embarrassed, he quickly turned away to his right, and made his way to the locker room, less confident than ever about defeating his quarry.

Chip was waiting for him as he made his way back into the gym. He had half of the court all to himself, and was taking, and making, shot after shot from outside the three-point stripe, much to the admiration of the dozen-or-so guys hanging around. He didn't look much like a basketball player, older and graying at the temples, a little shorter than Paul with a bit of a gut. But a player he was, as the other guys would readily testify, each having been pummeled by him in short order over the last couple of days.

"Whazzup, old man!" Paul said to him.

"It's about time," Chip replied, tossing him the ball a little harder than expected. "I thought you wimped out on me."

Paul took a shot and made it. "No way, José. I live for these games." He went and got the ball he had just shot, threw it to Chip even harder, and nodded in the direction of the guys waiting in the wings. "Finally got those cheerleaders you've been dreaming of, eh?"

Chip took a shot from well beyond the three-point stripe, and swished it. "I thought they were your sisters."

Paul grabbed the ball, and walked toward Chip. "Hey, man... don't dis my sister... I *will* take you out," he teased.

Chip ignored him. "You talk to much. I've got some new moves to terrorize you with."

Paul handed him the ball. "You don't scare me. And out of respect for my elders, I'll even let you have the ball first."

"Sixteen by ones, win by two," Chip determined.

"Go for it," Paul said in a Mafioso-style voice, crouching in a defensive posture.

With an instant dribble to the right, followed by a crossover dribble to his left, Chip breezed by Paul for an easy lay-up. Indeed, Chip was a great basketball player, but Paul was determined, and that kept him equal to the task. The game was close, Chip holding a narrow 12–11 lead. Paul had the ball. He faked left, then went right and had Chip beat for the tying score when he saw her again—the blonde from the aerobics class. She had come into the gym after the class ended, and had been watching them for some time.

GIRL OF MY DREAMS

Paul's vision locked in on her as he was going in for the lay-up, which had a disastrous effect on the shot, and Paul. The ball hit the bottom of the backboard, and bounced right back into his face as he slammed into the post the basket rested on. He stumbled to the surface of the track that encircled the court, and all the guys watching the game broke out laughing and high-fiving each other. With all the pride he could muster, he sat up on the floor and tried to gather himself together.

Britne suppressed her laughter and went to retrieve the ball. Chip walked over to Paul on the floor, watching Britne all the way, noticing that she was flat-out gorgeous. He was giving her the once over as he addressed Paul.

"Whoa, cowboy. You okay?"

Paul was looking at Britne as well, rubbing his shoulder, which was already throbbing with pain. "Right now, I don't feel a thing."

Chip turned his full attention to Paul. "Concentrate, man."

"Dude," Paul responded, still watching as Britne bent over to pick up the ball, "I *was* concentrating."

Chip reached out his hand and grasped ahold of Paul's, helping to pull him to his feet. "On the game, Paul… on the game."

"Whatever," Paul quipped back, with a smile on his face. "Time, okay?"

"Not too long, eh," Chip acquiesced, knowing that the hard-fought battle they were waging may have just become history.

Paul casually walked over to Britne, who was holding the ball and trying to spin it on her finger.

As he stopped in front of her, she smiled and handed him the ball. "Are you okay?"

"Oh yeah," Paul deadpanned, rolling his shoulders. "It's good for the back."

"You should be more careful out there. Bad enough you walk into doorways. Now this?" She used her towel to touch a small cut on his shoulder. "Maybe you need glasses."

"Nah…" Paul replied, trying to think of something clever to say. "Just blinded by your beauty."

"Flattery!" she said, pretending to fan herself.

"Honesty," he said back, thinking how corny he must sound.

She started to turn and walk away. Paul didn't realize it, but he started to follow. "Wait, what's your name?"

"What's yours?" she countered.

"Paul," he answered, offering his hand for a handshake.

She stopped and accepted the handshake. "Britne Nicole… my friends call me Britne."

"Very beautiful," he replied softly, pulling her hand to his lips and kissing it, "and so is your name."

She feigned irritability. "All charm, aren't you?"

"All yours, Britne Nicole," he replied in as suave a voice as he could make.

This brought a laugh from her, and an irritated voice from the court. "Hey, throw me the ball," Chip demanded.

Paul tossed the ball to Chip, and then turned his full attention immediately back to Britne.

"Your friend wants to play," she said.

"He can wait… destiny can't," Paul continued with his cliché bombardment.

"Enough already," she answered.

"What?"

"Just be real, please. Okay?"

"I am being real," Paul said, not quite so sure of it though.

"I'm just a simple, ordinary girl," she admitted, with truthful sincerity.

"Believe me, Britne, you're more than ordinary," Paul said in his own sincere honesty, which was not lost on her in the least.

"Thank you," she said, blushing. She offered him her hand once more. "It was nice meeting you, Paul."

He took her hand. "My pleasure."

She shook his hand, then pulled away and turned to walk off.

"Can I call you?" he asked, though she had her back to him.

"I don't think so," she responded, glancing over her shoulder, but continuing to walk away. "You'll see me around here."

She was getting a little farther away than Paul liked, so he again started after her, thinking to himself that this was just like a bad romance novel. "C'mon, wait a minute," he said as he caught up to her. "The girl of my dreams comes into my life, and you say, 'I'll see you around?' I just can't let that happen."

Britne was no pushover, which made her all the more attractive to Paul. "What do you want me to say," she replied.

"You could say you'll have dinner with me," Paul said, almost pleading.

Britne looked him over, and then looked deep into his eyes, feeling the fluttering of butterflies within her. "I'll tell you what," she said as they stopped, "I'm going to be at this club out on Damascus Road tonight. How about we meet there."

Paul's heart felt as if it stopped beating for a split second, and everything around him seemed brighter, but he did his best to hide the ecstasy he was experiencing.

"Interesting," he said with a smile.

"What's that?"

"You're the second person to mention that place to me today," Paul said.

Britne paused momentarily, waiting for his reply, then asked, "Well, what do you say?"

Paul was beaming. "Well... I made other plans already, but—for you—I'll change them."

"Good. I'll see you tonight then."

Paul's inner ecstasy became almost unbearable, and offered her his "puppy dog" look. "You're not gonna dump me, are you?"

Britne didn't quite see his plea for what it was. "Of course not. Why would you think that?"

Paul sensed he had offended her, feeling as vulnerable as he had ever felt, and figured the best thing to do was just be honest. Flashing her his best smile, he laid it all on the table for her to see. "Insecurities?"

She flashed the most brilliant and sincere smile he had ever seen, and Paul new he had said the right thing.

"I'll see you tonight," she said with a soft and gentle nod.

"Great!"

He watched her walk away, taking in her petite curves, swaying ever so perfectly. She seemed to skip out the door into the lobby, and he caught her actually taking one last glance over her shoulder before she disappeared.

Cloud nine was about twenty floors below his current elevation. He turned and headed back to the court, only to find Chip—and the rest of the circus—staring over at him with looks on their faces that made clear he wasn't going to live this down for a very long time.

Chip, knowing all too well what Paul was thinking at the moment, spoke as only a friend would speak. "I thought I lost you there," he said with a wink.

Grateful for his friend's sensitivity, Paul responded accordingly. "No way! I'm gonna whoop up on you, bud."

"Ha!" Chip bellowed, "not if there are baskets on the court."

"Bite me," Paul said as he swiped the ball from Chip's grasp and swished a jump shot from well beyond the three-point line.

Chip retrieved the ball as it bounced directly under the basket and casually turned to Paul. "You don't scare me!"

"Give me the ball, old man," Paul demanded with the motion of his hands, and the game resumed with Chip hurling the ball at his face. Paul played his best basketball ever; the funny thing was, he didn't notice, and didn't care one bit.

DISTRACTIONS

The house, a typical two-story all-brick design in a good neighborhood, wasn't overly huge. With stately aspects such as Roman-like columns, well-manicured landscaping complete with rose bushes and bonsais, and a beautiful green lawn, it was easy to see that good money was being spent for the home's upkeep.

Paul and Luc sauntered out of the house and headed for Luc's car, parked along the curb in front of the house. As usual, the late-model, teal Corvette had a new coat of wax on it, and the tires a new Armor-All treatment. Luc never went out in his baby without it looking or running show-room perfect. It was his pride and joy, and a source of considerable vanity.

"What a babe," Paul said as he neared the passenger side door.

"It cost me an arm and a leg," Luc agreed as he gave it an admiring look, standing across from Paul on the driver's side. "She is a beauty, though."

Paul gave him a funny look. "I wasn't talking about the car, Luc."

"Oh?" Luc questioned as he plopped himself into the cockpit with the authority of an ace fighter pilot.

"No," Paul continued as he opened the door and slid comfortably into the seat. "I was thinking about this chick I met today at the gym. Britne Nicole," he said with a slow, deep sigh.

"Jesus, her name even gets me breathing hard. Dude… there's something about this girl. I could feel it, right here." He tapped his heart emphatically. "She could, too. It showed in her eyes."

Luc said nothing at first. He just started the car, revved the engine a couple of times, and nudged it forward with the gentle touch of a new father holding his first-born son.

Paul was about to say something, when he was thrust against the back of his seat, Luc having launched his 'Vette with a burst of burning rubber, side-winding through the first block in a few short seconds. *This is insane,* Paul thought, wondering what would make Luc behave in such a way. This was his pride and joy, and he *never* mistreated her. Still pressed against the back, and holding on for his own sanity, he realized the street they were on had a sharp right turn coming up, and they weren't going to make it.

The white of Paul's eyes grew like a full moon in a cloudless sky, as their lives appeared to be coming to an abrupt end, when Luc cranked the steering wheel hard to the right and slammed his foot down hard on the brake, forcing the vehicle into a 360-degree spin at the edge of the bend in the road. The beautifully waxed and buffed Corvette was no longer the immaculate work of art Luc took so much pride in showing off, sitting there layered in dust from the cloud kicked up by his little circus act.

Paul threw his door open and jumped out with the vitriol of a man intent on taking vengeance on the first idiot that got in his way.

Luc opened his own door, and slowly stood by his prized possession, looking intently at his best friend.

Paul furiously spun around in his tracks, ready to lay into the man he'd come to rely upon so intimately.

"All the more reason to be cautious, Paul," Luc exhorted casually, before his friend could speak. "Especially now, after this morning. You can't let your guard down, not for one minute."

Paul was caught off guard, trembling in his fury. It was an awfully extreme way of making a point. Knowing full well what Luc was trying to say, he brushed aside the concern with an almost cavalier air, and blurted out his anger. "Hey, man! I'm not worried about this morning!"

Luc was flabbergasted. "Not worried? Dude, they almost blew you away!"

Paul shrugged it off as if it were nothing. "But they didn't," he said with conviction, staring straight into Luc's eyes.

Luc shook his head in disbelief, and gave his beautiful dust-covered 'Vette a quick once-over, then settled himself back into the driver's seat, slamming the door emphatically.

Paul leaned over and looked at his soul brother through the open passenger door, who sat there, silently, staring straight ahead, waiting for the next round to begin. With a deep, heavy sigh, he turned a full circle where he stood, looking everywhere… but nowhere in particular. Slowly he moved back to the car, stood by the door for another second or two, plopped himself into the passenger's seat and shut his door, looking straight ahead in the same way that Luc was doing. They sat there in silence.

Paul finally looked over at Luc, proclaiming, as if none of what had just transpired occurred, "And don't you find it ironic, that on the very same day, I meet the girl of my dreams? Yes, my good man, fate is calling, and she has blue eyes."

These two men knew each other, and shared a bond that was stronger than steel, but Luc was buying none of it.

"Let's just hope that fate doesn't trap you in some dead end alley with nowhere to turn."

"Yo, bro," Paul laughed. "Who was it telling me, just this morning, to lighten up?"

Luc rolled his eyes in disbelief, knowing that he was getting nowhere with the most stubborn, pig-headed man he had ever known. "That was earlier," he said with a sigh, "I talked to Billy this afternoon. He didn't have much good to say. He said that they just barely missed a bust on a shipment of Uzi-Twins." He glanced over at Paul, who was staring blankly out the passenger window. "Are you listening, a shipment of *Twins.* Paul, we can't go up against those. We got enough problems with their 44-Longnecks."

Paul was on an entirely different wavelength, one with a high drift rate. "By the way, we're not hitting the old standby tonight. We're heading out to Steve's new place, on Damascus Road."

Luc was in total disbelief. "Paul, did you hear a word I just said?"

Paul turned to him, and said emphatically, "*Yes…* I did. I just don't want to talk about it right now. Let it wait until tomorrow, okay? Please?"

Luc gave in, knowing the resolve of his good friend all too well. "All right, but let's hope tomorrow isn't too late."

"Thank you," Paul exclaimed, lifting his hands in mild celebration. "Now, let's go party. And one more thing," he said with a jestfully threatening point of his finger, "if you ever do that to me again, I'll personally beat…"

Before he could finish his claim for superiority, Luc once again floored the gas and spun the 'Vette in a full circle, then casually started to drive away, apologizing to his baby as they went.

THE CLUB

The ride to the party was quiet. Paul was self-absorbed in the thrill and anticipation of seeing Britne again, and Luc was equally absorbed in worries about the day's events. And Paul's nonchalance *toward* them. Paul always had a casual attitude about danger, Luc thought, but now he was infatuated and distracted. It was the last thing they needed, yet his love and adoration for this man who had saved his own life, on many occasions, compelled him to want to share in this moment. He had never seen Paul so happy, and he was not about to interfere. No, Luc thought, he'll just guard his friend's back, like usual.

After what seemed an eternity to Paul, they reached their destination, only to have to wait in a line just to enter the packed parking lot. Inching along toward the entrance, he scanned left and right, thinking to himself that Steve had hit a gold mine; it was as busy as any place he'd ever seen.

Finally gaining access to the property, Luc circled the lot a few times until he was able to find a suitable spot to showcase his high-end toy; two empty spaces adjacent to each other in the farthest corner, some hundred yards from the club's front doors. Backing in so as to occupy both spaces, he turned off the vehicle.

Paul found himself gazing at Luc, dismayed at the lengths to which his friend would travel just to protect a paint job. With a smirk on his face and a shake of his head, he hastily exited the 'Vette and made a beeline toward the building.

This adolescent infatuation of Paul's was both humorous and frustrating to Luc. Like so often before, his eyes became Paul's eyes as well, surveying the lot for any signs of danger and the most expeditious route of escape should the need arise unexpectedly. One day, he thought, Paul was going to find himself alone and in a world of hurt because of his lackadaisical attitude. This, of course, motivated Luc to quicken his pace and catch up to his most trusted confidant.

Paul wasn't totally oblivious to his behavior, and was waiting for Luc at the front entrance to the club. Making their way inside, it was impossible not to notice the size of the crowd packed together like sardines in a can. But something was different about this place. The air was fresh and clean, and the patrons seemed very friendly and open, not like most clubs where they have to practically threaten someone to move out of their way. Everyone was greeting everyone, shaking hands and even hugging at times. A band was playing on the stage against the wall across the room, and the crowd was totally grooving with the music. Slowly they weaved through the crowd toward the bar to their right, and Paul became acutely aware of the tremendous solo that the guitarist was playing, an amazing, almost hypnotizing, mastery of the classical scales.

"This place is packed," Paul yelled to Luc, trying to make himself heard over the music and noise of the crowd. "I'm impressed."

"Did you expect any less from Steve?" Luc responded almost inaudibly.

Paul could only shrug his shoulders in pseudo agreement. "Whatever he does," Luc continued, "he always seems to do it right."

They finally managed to reach the bar, and Luc was in the mood to help his brother-in-arms loosen up a bit. "My treat, bro," he offered, leaning against the bar.

"Cool, I'll take a Corona, extra lime." Paul leaned back against the bar and watched the band, impressed with the music but not quite understanding the lyrics. He recognized the band, though, as the one from the CD.

Luc flagged down the bartender to order their refreshments. "Two Coronas, one with extra lime, please," he requested, surprised at himself for saying "please." He had never done that in a bar before.

The bartender gave him a serious look. "Sorry, sir, no alcohol," he said authoritatively.

"No brew? You gotta be kidding me!" Luc said somewhat shocked.

The bartender smiled at him. "No brew, nothing alcoholic."

Luc hit Paul on the shoulder to get his attention. " Hey, did you hear that?"

"What?" he said without turning away from the stage, still transfixed on the guitarist.

"This place is dry—no alcohol!"

This got Paul's attention, and he turned to question the bartender. "None?"

"Sorry," the bartender returned with a polite and sincere smile, obviously used to this kind of surprised reaction from many of the patrons.

Paul took notice of the tablets on the wall behind the bar. *The Ten Commandments? Yes,* he thought, *this place is very different,* and he began to understand that Steve was very serious about what he had told him earlier that morning.

"That figures," Paul said to Luc, disappointed and nodding toward the stone tablets above them on the wall.

"Give me a Mountain Dew then," he told the bartender.

"Make that two," Luc said, still a bit shocked, staring up at the Commandments.

"These guys are great," Paul said to Luc, turning his attention back to the band. "That guitarist *rocks*."

"So… do… they," Luc replied, referring to the girls walking by them.

"Down, boy!" Paul laughed.

The guitarist finished his solo, and the song wrapped up in grand fashion, sending the crowd into an appreciative frenzy. Leading the cheers was none other than Paul himself.

"All right," the singer announced, "Billy Echols on guitar. He's great, isn't he?" The crowd went into another frenzy. "This next song," he continued, "is about why many of us are here tonight. Its called 'Searchin' for Love.'" The crowd gave them one more round of applause as they began the song.

At the same time, the sodas arrived from the bartender.

Luc grabbed the Dews and handed one to Paul. "Here you go, man. Party down!"

Paul laughed at the irony of partying with Mountain Dew. "Oh yeah, party down. Man, that guy on guitar is great!"

Luc laughed with him, and then excused himself. "I'm going sightseeing," he said with a nod, and disappeared into the crowd.

Paul just listened to the song, one he recognized from listening to the CD. It was a hard-groovin', funky rock song, and he couldn't help noticing how those in the crowd were all bobbing their heads and shoulders in unison…

Music was a'rockin' in a dim lit bar.
Women dressed t'kill, as the men looked on.
   Loneliness filled the air
   Searchin' for someone to care
Women strut their stuff just to catch an eye.
Men take the bait as they fantasize
   Wanting love to share
   Searchin' in despair.

Searchin' for love
   in the middle of the night.
Searchin' for love with no end in sight.
Searchin' for love
   to fill your empty heart.
Searchin'… for love.

Paul was doing some sightseeing of his own from the bar, knowing that if he stood at a focal point in a club like this, he could observe just about anything, or anyone. It was the "anyone" he was most anxious to see. He spent the time split between watching the band and watching the people passing by the bar.

The emptiness you feel deep down inside.
Won't get filled with rendezvous' at night.
   Searchin' for true love
   Accept his from above.
Many of you know what I'm talkin' about
Do you want to turn your life around?
   Hope is in the air
   Jesus really cares.

Searchin' for love
   in the middle of the night.
Searchin' for love with no end in sight.

Searchin' for love
to fill your empty heart.
Searchin'… for love.

As the guitarist was finishing another terrific solo, the crowd roared their deafening approval. When they parted a bit, there she was, looking all the more beautiful dressed for clubbing. Steve was with her, he noted, but it didn't matter. His feet moved on their own, and as he approached them, her eyes made contact with his, nearly taking his breath away.

Steve saw Paul, and addressed him immediately. "Paul! Wow, I didn't expect to see you in here so soon."

"I didn't plan on it, actually," Paul said, looking over at Britne. "I was sort of invited."

The eye contact between the two didn't go unnoticed by Steve, who was acutely sensitive to protecting his sister. He wasn't at all comfortable with the way Paul was looking at Britne or the gleam in his little sister's eyes as she returned his gaze.

"Oh, this is my sister, Britne," he introduced, strictly out of respect and courtesy. "Britne… Paul. Paul and I are… old friends."

Paul wasn't at all prepared for this new information, and instantly the euphoria he had been riding evaporated, and panic filled the void. "Your sister," he exclaimed with a bit too much protest, "I didn't know you had a sister!"

"Actually, she's my half sister," Steve explained. "She came with me when I moved back." He gave Britne the best 'scolding, older-brother' look he could muster. "I tried to talk her out of it, but—"

"But I'm my own woman," Britne interrupted without hesitation, trying to reassure Paul of her own independence with tender, but direct, eye contact.

"I'm sure you are," Paul agreed with a smile.

Steve waved to someone in the crowd. "There's someone I need to talk to over there. I'll talk to you later, Paul." He turned to Britne. "Be good."

As he walked away, Paul asked, "So, he's your brother?"

Britne corrected him. "Half brother, but we're very close. He's very protective."

"Great," Paul said. "I'll keep that in mind."

"You have a problem with that?" Britne asked, unsure of what he was implying and fighting off the irritation that was growing inside of her. This wasn't what she had been looking forward to all afternoon.

At the same time, Paul felt immediately on the defensive. "No, but I'm sure *he* will."

"Excuse me?" Britne replied sharply.

"Steve and I go back a ways. Not all good." Things were moving in the wrong direction. Subconsciously he began to look around, as if searching for an escape route. Taking notice of the bar once again, he thought of a way to change the subject, if only for a second. "You thirsty?" he asked her.

LOVE

Britne, too, wanted a way out of this conversation, and saw the gesture for what it was. "Sure," she replied, grateful not to be continuing that line of thought.

The short walk to the bar was silent between them, the music and crowd notwithstanding, and served to relieve some of the tension that had built between them.

As they approached the bar, Britne leaned over and gently touched Paul's arm with her hand, breaking the thin layer of ice that had formed. "Actually, I got the feeling that's how it was," she admitted to him.

The gentle caress of her fingers on his skin wasn't lost on Paul, and his heart softened even more to the beauty of this woman next to him. But her admission surprised him a bit.

"How's that?" he inquired.

Britne replied, "Steve was waiting for me at the club, earlier, and made some vague comments about your motorcycle. Well, what he said was that it belonged to a guy named Paul he knew, and that I should try to avoid him. I wondered if the person he was talking about might just have been you."

They arrived at the bar and Paul signaled for two more soft drinks. He attempted to make light of things, metaphorically. "So, now you have this warped image of me," he said, trying desperately not to sound defeated, and continued with a cheesy, but gentlemanly, bow, "The knight in rusty armor, m'lady."

Britne let out a courtesy chuckle. In contrast to the picture that Steve had painted of Paul, she could see beneath the surface of this man a tenderhearted romantic. She liked that very much. He also seemed to be very sensitive, and his earlier confession of insecurities at the gym was probably truer than he even realized himself.

"Hold on a minute," she rebutted. "He might not agree with what you do, but he still values your friendship." She paused a bit, and then let out a sigh. "Besides, we don't see eye to eye on everything."

Paul's interest, and pride, was piqued at this admission, and he found himself searching for more. "Oh, yeah!"

Britne offered some clarification. "I don't like what you do, either, but, at least you're *trying* to do something positive."

This struck a chord with Paul, and he got very serious all of a sudden. He found himself opening up to her and sharing doubts that he didn't know resided within him.

"I'm not so sure of that, anymore. I did a lot of thinking when Steve left. A lot! But, I just can't pull myself away from all of this stuff like he did. It's personal, and I feel obligated. I can't rest for one minute. Not until this is stopped." He paused a bit, looking down at the floor. "Maybe he's right. Maybe I *am* trapped by hatred or anger or… I don't know."

He shook his head slightly, unconsciously, questioning himself more than ever before.

Britne looked at him, hoping he would lift his eyes to hers. She could see the pain he must be feeling, but couldn't understand why he was taking this all so personally. Her heart went out to him at that, and she reached over and rested her hand on his forearm. Her words were filled with genuine care and sincerity.

"Just follow your heart, Paul. If you do that, everything will work out."

His skin, and heart, tingled at her touch once again; and her voice, soft and tender as it was, brought a smile to his face. *Today, he thought, is certainly turning out to be one of the strangest, and most coincidental, days of my life.* Something was going on, and he hadn't a clue what it was. He looked into her eyes, now, and found himself lost in a sea of blue tranquility, rescued from the torment of his own thoughts.

He remembered what he had told Missy earlier that day. "You know, I said the same thing to my sister this morning."

She smiled at him warmly, and he turned around to watch the band some. They were both leaning against the bar when the band made a subtle, but dramatic, segue from their rocking fast pace into a slow song. Paul didn't recognize it at all, but looking over at Britne, he could see that she very clearly did; tilting her head backwards, with her eyes closed, she seemed to be absorbing it all in. The slow, melodic downbeat of the piano, in contrast to the beautiful, high male tenor voice.

Paul couldn't stop looking at this most beautiful of women standing next to him. Her cascading golden tresses as they fell over the slope of her neck and shoulders. Fleeting thoughts of his recent conversation with Luc skipped across his mind, only to be washed away with a torrent of feelings for this… this Angel… feelings he hadn't felt in forever.

She tilted her head toward him, and opened her eyes, catching him totally by surprise. He felt like a little child stealing from the cookie jar, and looked away from her instinctively. Embarrassed, but unable to resist his heart, he looked back, only to find that she was still gazing in his direction. And she smiled. Not a big smile, but a tender one, the corners of her mouth just tipping upward. He smiled back, and she very slowly turned her attention to the band again. It was agonizing for Paul, who wanted to get close to her. Finally, after a few seconds of debating within himself, he leaned toward her.

"Would you like to dance?" he asked.

She looked down, as he had done earlier. "I don't think so," she answered somewhat timidly, "but… thank you."

For all of his bravado, Paul was never too aggressive with women. Not even growing up, in school, when all the girls hung around him and his band. Tonight, though, this was different. There was something unique and wonderful about Britne; beautiful, feisty, intelligent, independent. But there was something else he couldn't put his finger on, something different about her. And he knew he was in deep, deep trouble.

He had no choice but to surrender. He persisted. "I won't bite, Brit," he gently implored, smiling and offering his hand to her.

"It's just that," she started to say, then looked up at him, offering him the most beautiful smile, and without further resistance surrendered just the same. "Sure, I'd like to."

She put her hand into his, and they slowly weaved their way through the crowd. Arriving at the floor, he turned to her and tentatively took her into his arms, resting his hands in the small of her back. At first the dance was awkward, and Britne seemed totally out of her element. Slowly, timidly, she eventually rested her head on his right shoulder, and he took her right hand into his left and rested it next to his heart. And they danced. The smell of her hair calmed him. And they danced.

Across the club, a couple of disappointed eyes watched the whole thing unfold, from conversation to dance. They belonged to Steve. He watched it all, saw what was happening, and knew then and there that he had a problem on his hands. He also knew there wasn't much he could do about it. Love at first sight… what a stupid thing it was. He wasn't oblivious to the wonderful gift the Lord had given humanity, the ability to love and be in love. But love at first sight, that was a totally different beast, and Steve didn't look forward to the pain that Britne was probably going to suffer. His baby sister, falling for the man who was once his best friend; a man surrounded by danger and turmoil. He'd been there, he'd lived it, and he *knew* it. He wasn't quite sure how, but one thing was certain: somehow, some way, this had to be stopped. His thoughts rambled on. Panic was knocking on the door of his mind. And he watched.

Paul, for the first time in recent memory, was at peace, and this scared him because he knew this was not his reality, and it would find a way of leaving a hole in his heart. The prospect of a relationship in his life with a woman like Britne didn't scare him. But the idea that anything in his life might bring harm to her— that did. It petrified him. But for now, the sweet vanilla scent of her perfume, or shampoo, whatever it was, gave him a deep sense of peace. So engrossed by this moment, like an oasis that brought to his life refreshment and rest, he just barely caught the words she whispered into his ear. He didn't know what they meant, but was sure they were important. He would find out later. All he knew was that he didn't want this moment to stop… this feeling… this peace.

He had called her Brit. In doing so, he gained access to the one place in her heart that very few ever got near. He didn't know it. How could he? Memories flooded her mind, and a tear formed in her eye. They were happy memories, though. Images of her life before all hell broke loose in the world. He had to know. She had to somehow allow him to share this deeply buried haven in her heart. Lifting her head from his shoulder, she spoke softly into his ear.

"My mother used to call me 'Brit,' when she was alive."

That was all she said, and laid her head back on his shoulder. And she smiled. Eventually, that lone tear finally escaped and edged its way down the crest of her nose, dropping to be absorbed into the material of his shirt. And she rested there, her head on his shoulder. And they danced.

As the song came to an end, Britne pulled away from him, a bit flustered. "Could we get some fresh air, please?" she asked him as they stood there on the dance floor.

Paul looked into her eyes, and smiled.

"Sure."

As they were leaving, Paul could sense something deep within Britne, and a heightened awareness of something else, far beyond the two of them. He chastised himself for any physical thoughts he may have had when they were dancing. These feelings, these thoughts, they were all so new to his way of thinking, and he didn't know what to make of them. *Today has absolutely turned out to be the strangest day of my life,* he again thought to himself.

The air outside was cool and fresh. Silence gripped the two of them as they walked through the parking lot. But it wasn't the kind that makes one uncomfortable or nervous. No, this was the kind that words would never be able to fill, for the silence itself spoke of an intimate kind of closeness. Words, actually, were the enemy of this kind of moment.

Paul tenderly reached over and slipped his fingers between hers. And she accepted them.

"Sorry if I upset you in there," Paul said, looking off into the dark distance.

"You didn't upset me. What gave you that idea?"

"When I called you 'Brit,'" Paul explained.

"Oh, don't worry about that," Britne said. "To be honest, it made me feel good. It was my mom's nick name for me growing up. She used to act like she was mad if anyone else called me by that name." She chuckled to herself. "Its funny, I know… but as a child, those kind of things have a lot of personal meaning. She'd point her finger at the other people, make a funny face, and say, 'Don't you dare call her that. Only I'm allowed to.' Then she'd wink at me. Steve—what a goof—he'd tease her by saying it a couple of times behind her back, then he'd run away."

By now they ended up at Luc's car, and leaned against the driver's side door. "You said something about 'when she was alive'?" Paul asked.

"Yeah, she died about ten years ago, on my birthday ironically. Actually, she and daddy were both killed… in a bombing. It happens everywhere, you know. They were out picking up my present…" She stopped short right there.

Paul waited silently for her to continue, but she didn't. He felt a sadness about bringing up the subject. "I'm sorry, I shouldn't have asked."

Britne looked at him. "Please, don't be sorry. Sometimes it hurts more than others, but it helps to talk about it."

Paul took a few steps away, and tried to change the subject. "I never knew Steve had a sister."

"I guess he tried to forget it all," she replied. "We moved in with my daddy's sister after that. We had the same mom, and so, being twenty and not related to anyone but me, he decided to leave. Said he had to find himself." She stopped for a second, then continued, looking down at the ground. "I missed him a lot. When he came home, I decided not to ever lose touch with him again. That's why I came with him."

Paul came closer to her, and gently lifted her chin. "I'm really glad you did, Brit." He leaned in and tried to kiss her, but she turned away from him at the last second, and took a few steps away.

"You know that song we danced to?" she asked with her back to him.

Paul was cursing himself for being so stupid. Still, he felt she wanted to kiss him, and tried to recover the moment, and think of something clever to say, something she might want to hear and perhaps gain a second chance. "It was beautiful… just like you."

Britne let the platitude go. "It's my favorite song. It's a love song, you know, about, well, eternal love," she said, turning to face him. "About God's lo—"

TONY

The screeching of tires, and the roar of a bored-out big-block engine, grabbed his attention like a Pit Bull on a broken chain. He immediately recognized that sound, and looked up to see the pitch black, late model Dodge Ram pickup he'd encountered all too many times—more than ever recently—swerving around the turn at the front of the street, some two hundred yards away.

Instinctively he reached for his gun packed tightly against his left side. It wasn't there! In his haste to get to the club and meet Britne, he must have left it.

"Go inside," he commanded, running around to the passenger side and opening the door.

"Who's that?" She asked.

"Go inside, Brit... *now!*" he yelled over the top of the 'Vette.

The look in Paul's eyes spoke volumes of the danger that now existed, and she remembered some of the things Steve had told her. Turning, she sprinted as fast as she could down the length of the parking lane, and then toward the building. Paul, on the other hand, started rummaging through, around and under the front seats as the sound of the truck's revving Hemi quickly approached. "Come on, Come on," he mumbled over and over, glimpsing through the rear window to see the truck closing in. Finally he found what he was after—a pistol. It was much lighter than the cannon he usually carried, but it would have to do. He looked up again to see the Ram whip past him toward the parking lot entrance, and he jumped out of the car and bolted across the lot, bounding atop the hoods and roofs of the various and sundry vehicles blocking his path.

In the meantime, a stir was going on inside the club as Britne came running in screaming for Steve, who was all the way across the floor, to the far right of the stage, talking to the singer of the band. The crowd parted like the Red Sea, which promptly caught the attention of Luc, who was upstairs having a friendly conversation with a beautiful young brunette in a bright red dress. He knew immediately that trouble was brewing, and watched as Britne approached her brother and pointed outside excitedly. After years of this kind of living, his instincts took over, and he pulled out his gun and sprinted down the stairs, two and three at a time, slamming through the doors to join Paul outside.

The Ram entered the lot squealing and swerving, spewing rock and dust everywhere. Paul continued to hurdle and race, the cars before him becoming steeplechase obstacles. The truck was just to his left now, as he leapt from the last car between him and the club. The Ram skidded to rest some fifty feet from the entrance, as Paul came to a sliding stop between it and the doors. Arms outstretched, the pistol held at eye level bearing down on the occupants of the truck, Paul served as the only impedance to their wrecking havoc on the occupants inside.

"Stay in the truck, Tony," Paul warned.

Luc, having just exited the building with his own gun leveled and aimed in the direction of the Dodge, sidled up next to Paul without uttering a word. Once again, they had each other's back.

Simultaneously, exiting the passenger side of the truck was Tony, a short, stocky man in his late twenties with dark, wavy hair and deep blue eyes set ablaze with a fire of hatred. The two men who greeted Paul that morning were with him in the truck. One stepped out of the passenger side, partially guarded by the front end of the Ram, while the other slipped through the window in the back of the truck's cab, taking a position behind the cab itself.

Luc quickly shifted to Paul's left, and altered his aim between the man on the ground and the one in the bed of the truck. With the most obvious of gestures he kept Tony's friends at bay. Words weren't necessary to communicate the alternative between life and death, should he lose sight of their hands.

There was no time to think, as things escalated, reaching a tumultuous boiling point—getting very ugly, very fast. By now Steve, Britne, and many of the crowd had exited the building and gathered behind Paul and Luc, watching the events unfold.

"Get out of my way, 'cause I'm going in," Tony howled, consumed with rage.

Paul, surprisingly calm amidst the high tension, tried to reason with him. "Come on, Tony. Just get back in the truck and leave."

Tony was in no mood to negotiate, and tried to push past him. "I said, *get out of my—*"

He was cut short by Paul's right elbow, smashed squarely and violently into his face, snapping his head backward and lifting his feet six inches into the air. He hit the ground flat on his back.

Paul moved like lightning and, before Tony could gain his senses, was kneeling next to him, thrusting the pistol's barrel against his brother's throat. His right knee firmly pressed Tony's right hand flat to the ground to keep it immobilized.

Tony's buddies tried to react, but Luc was faster, firing a shot that ricocheted off the roof of the truck, and sliding around the front end to face them at point blank range.

They stopped moving.

"Don't do this, Tony," Paul threatened in a confident, steady voice.

Tony was in no position to do anything at the moment, and neither were his cohorts. He stared into the steel brown eyes of his older brother, but his anger spoke for him nonetheless.

"I'm gonna hunt you down like a wild dog."

"Yeah, well… I bite," Paul said without flinching. He casually stood to his feet, directly over his younger sibling, his gun still aimed at his head.

Luc was still focused on the other two men, shifting his aim between them accordingly.

Tony gingerly climbed to his feet, wiped himself off, gained control of his balance, and spit a mouthful of blood at Paul's feet. Moving ever so cautiously toward his brother, he slowly put the tip of his right index finger on the barrel of the gun pointed at his head, and pulled it down to his heart. The two of them stood there, staring into each other's eyes, neither one blinking or flinching.

Tony turned, and headed for the passenger side of the Ram. "Let's Go," he instructed his subordinates. The man on the passenger side slid into the truck, while the other leapt over the side of the bed, landing just in front of Paul, then climbed into the driver's seat. Tony paused at his door and stared at the crowd behind Paul.

"Nice place, Steve," he said, voice laced with sarcasm. "Just remember… some people play the blues." He got in and slammed his door shut.

The truck's engine roared to life, the driver flooring the gas pedal for dramatic emphasis. He then inched the truck forward, staring at Paul with nothing but cold, soulless eyes. Tony stared at Luc as they moved past.

Luc cautiously backed away from the truck, keeping his aim on Tony's head, as the Ram moved toward the parking lot exit at a snail's pace. At the exit, the driver floored the gas and brakes at the same time, kicking up a huge gray cloud that rose a hundred feet, filling the air with the stench of burning rubber. Then they peeled off and went speeding down the road.

Paul couldn't help but notice the police cruiser parked along the road about a hundred yards away... waiting... watching. He snickered in Luc's direction to get his attention, and nodded toward the cruiser. Luc saw it, too.

A collective sigh of relief came over the crowd, and most made their way back into the club with a murmur of excitement surrounding them all.

Steve didn't share that relief, though. He knew better. This wasn't over. It was just the beginning.

There were four still left outside. Paul and Luc stood out front and continued to watch the departed truck. Steve and Britne were lingering by the doors.

Steve sauntered up to Paul's left side. "You would've killed him, wouldn't you," he spoke softly, turning to look him square in the eyes.

Paul, nonplused, looked at his pistol, then at Steve.

"To be honest," he said, raising the gun to bear on Steve's chest, "I try to avoid it." He pulled the trigger, ejecting a long stream of water, planting a huge spot on Steve's shirt. Steve gasped and looked down at his chest, then clenched his fists angrily.

"You're out of your mind, you know that?" Luc said to Paul over is right shoulder.

"Hey, it's all I could find in the car," Paul apologized with a slight smile. "Looks real enough, though." He turned to go back inside the club. "Where *did* you get this weapon of mass hydration?" he asked, squirting Luc in the crotch.

Luc tried to turn away quickly, but wasn't fast enough. "Dude, man!" he exclaimed, trying to wipe away the spot in his pants. Then it dawned on him that Paul didn't have his own gun.

"Where'd you—"

"Your car."

"How'd you—"

"I didn't lock my door."

"Paul!"

"Habit, man. Good thing, too," he said, looking over his shoulder at Luc while reaching for the door. Turning to head inside, he ran into the door, just like at the gym. "Son of a…" he exclaimed.

Luc laughed out loud, as much at the guffaw as it was a release of all the tension. "You really do need those glasses."

Paul ignored him, stopped, turned to face Britne, and reached out his hand for hers.

She paused and looked at Steve, who wasn't paying any attention to them. That's when she knew she wanted to be with this man, took his hand, and walked inside with him.

Steve was alone, now. Just him and his thoughts. He knew this would happen, eventually. It always did when a man proclaimed the truth. He also knew it wouldn't be easy. So, he just stood there by himself, gazing deep into the star-filled heavens. *What a beautiful night,* he thought, as he offered a prayer of thanksgiving to the Lord, while asking for strength and courage. And peace filled his heart. With a deep, long sigh, he turned to head back inside the club and tend to the needs of his patrons.

It had finally begun.

THOUGHTS

Reality has a funny way of forcing us to stand up and account for our lives. Often, we try to run from our problems, but that never works. Eventually, we come to realize there's no way to avoid dealing with them...

LIFE

It was raining cats and dogs, and thunder rolled across the dark gray sky like waves crashing to the shore. The parking lot of the pizzeria was nearly empty, as most normal folks had chosen to stay in, protected from the elements whipping about outside. Adjacent to the road that ran past the front of the property, a simple square sign read in black lettering, "Doreen's Place," against a lavender backdrop bordered by Italian olive branches. The building was a small, single story square about the size of a typical single family dwelling.

An older couple, a husband and wife that probably lived in the surrounding neighborhood, jogged across the parking lot and entered the main portico to the diner. It was a casual little bistro, and a sign at the door read, "Please be seated. Help yourself to the endless buffet."

In the middle of the café was a fairly decent food bar, covered by a fake wood roof, filled with every kind of Italian food one could hope to find, and the obligatory salad offerings.

Surrounding the food bar were about twenty tables, one of which the older couple promptly claimed for themselves. Along the left side of the building, about a dozen padded booths lined the front and side walls. In the corner booth, Missy was sitting in solitude, a lone beverage perched on the table in front of her.

Wearing a set of headphones, she was listening to music in the CD player that was resting next to the dark red plastic tumbler. Her eyes were closed, and she was holding in her hands the *Damascus Road* CD that Paul had received from Steve not long ago.

Waiting for Mark to arrive, she found herself listening over and over to a particular song that was intimately apropos to her dilemma. Mark was running very late, which wasn't like him at all, and she was beginning to worry.

The song ended, and she hit the replay button for the fifth or sixth time. It was a beautiful song, she thought, with a flowing melodic acoustic guitar, accented by an electric guitar lead here and there. The voice was nice, and soft. She listened, and as she'd done many times already, she cried; tears of confusion, tears of struggle, tears of doubt. But she listened, and the words spoke to the deepest part of her soul, and helped her understand the answers to the questions that she struggled with. Sitting there, listening to this song, she knew what she was to do…

> *Sitting in the corner,*
> *Thinkin' 'bout your life restlessly.*
> *Watching all your dreams*
> *Pass before your eyes endlessly.*
> *Questioning yourself -*
>   *Why did this have to be?*
> *Asking yourself -*
>   *Was it worth the ecstasy?*
>
> *Don't crush the seed—*
>   *A flower of innocence.*
> *Don't crush the seed -*
>   *The beauty of life.*
> *You have a chance,*
>   *To rescue the innocent.*
> *Don't crush the seed -*
>   *No, please… don't end this life.*

Mark showed up and quietly sat down across from Missy. He began to speak to her, but she lifted her finger to her mouth in a silencing gesture, never opening her eyes. She just listened. And the tears kept flowing.

Mark was worried. Why was she crying the way she was? Did he hurt her *that* much by being late? He noticed the CD case she was holding and it had a picture on the front of the sign that stood over Steve's place. That was odd, he thought. She didn't look at him, but listened to the song until it was done…

> *Sharing with each other*
> *The only kind of love that you know.*
> *Promising each other*
> *This love of yours will never grow old.*
>   *Now, you share the gift of life –*
> *A miracle to see.*
>   *But you ask yourself –*
> *should I end this life… secretly.*
>
>   *Don't crush the seed –*
>   *A flower of innocence.*
>   *Don't crush the seed –*
>   *The beauty of life.*
>   *You have a chance,*
>   *To rescue the innocent.*
>   *Don't crush the seed –*
>   *No, please… don't end this life*

When the song ended, Missy opened her eyes, removed the headphones, and turned off the CD player. Reaching across the table, she rested her hand on Mark's, and smiled. Then they talked.

It was a long talk, and at first Mark was shaken. He wasn't ready for this at all. They were both so young, he thought. But they *did* talk, and it wasn't long before the heaviness had lifted. They started to laugh, and their once hopeless future took on new meaning for both of them. The tears of confusion Missy had been shedding were replaced by tears of joy. And Mark, he cried, too. The same tears of joy. Life could be strangely uplifting, and a new life was the most uplifting thing any person could experience.

He moved over to the other side of the booth and sat next to the woman he loved deeper than his own life. And she loved him. He could no longer contain himself. He was going to be a father! He put his arm around her shoulders, and she laid her head on his, and they sat there together, both dreaming of the family they'd soon be sharing together. They talked some more, and eventually left the restaurant hand in hand, moving into their future knowing that whatever came their way, they'd be able to handle it all... together.

CHOICES

For the last couple of weeks, Steve had seen less and less of Britne. And when he actually *had* seen her, she was usually with Paul.

As of late, life was rather uneventful. The club was busier than he'd anticipated, and many lives were impacted in a positive way because of the work he was doing. On the surface, one could easily conclude the truth he was trying to share was reaping dividends in changed lives, but he wasn't about to let his guard down. Something was in the air, and he knew this was probably the proverbial "calm before the storm." It was only a matter of time before Tony and his band of thugs stepped up their activity.

That thought, in and of itself, was enough for Steve to feel it necessary to have a talk with Britne. In the rare times she wasn't with Paul, she was giddy, humming songs, and staring off into space with a silly grin on her face… all the tell-tale signs of being in love.

This day was different, though, and Steve finally had some quality time alone with her. He'd asked for her help a few days ago to do some cleaning at the club. At first he figured she just blew him off because there was no sign of her. But she finally found, or made, the time to lend a helping hand. Most of the morning was spent working hard, with an uncomfortable silence hovering between them. This went on for hours, and Steve could no longer refrain from addressing the serious concerns that lay on his heart.

They were taking a break, and he was sitting on a pool table next to a window. She was leaning against the frame of the side door, staring into the deluge of rain that was pouring down outside.

"So," he said, finally breaking the silence, "you and Paul seem pretty close these days."

She didn't respond.

"I hardly see you any more, Brit. How are things going?" He asked, meaning "with you and Paul."

The last thing she wanted was to have this conversation, and she didn't say anything for a few minutes. It surprised her that Steve was letting her silence go. It wasn't his nature to do so. Knowing he *really* wanted to talk was making her feel guilty, though. She loved Steve very much, and owed him at least an effort at communicating. It was difficult to find the right words, so she just blurted out the first intelligent sentence that she could muster.

"I hate this weather."

"Don't change the subject, Brit."

"All I said was I hated the weather."

"Yeah, I know what you *said*. But why do you always change the subject when I bring up you and Paul, which, I say again, isn't often… 'cause I never see you anymore." His voice had a sharp edge to it.

"That's because I know what you're going to say, and I don't want to hear it." Her voice was taking on an edge of its own.

Steve had hoped she might be more willing to discuss the issue, but her usual candor and independence was grating on his nerves. Pulling a cigarette from his pocket and lighting it, he continued.

"He's not like us, Britne."

Britne was genuinely ticked off at the sight of the cigarette, and took it from his hand with a little more force than expected, then tossed it out into the rain. .

"Some people would say *you're* not a Christian because you smoke those wretched things, and we both know that's not true."

Steve was on the defensive now, but still emphatic. "You know what I'm saying. He's not a believer, not in his heart."

Britne was irritated, but knew in her own heart that he was right. Still, she wasn't about to let him know that.

"How do you know what's in his heart? You don't even know what's in your own heart. Only God knows a man's heart."

"Just look at his—"

Britne cut him off harshly. "I don't want to talk about this, Paul."

"Steve, remember?"

"What?"

"You called me Paul," he pointed out.

"Sorry."

Once again, silence overtook them. Clearly things were more serious than he had thought. He had to know something. "You *love* him, don't you?"

Britne looked at the floor. "I don't know."

"Look, sis, I just don't want you to get hurt."

Britne held her gaze at the floor. "He makes me feel so good, Steve, like I'm the most important person in the world to him. I've never felt this way before."

Things were *far* more serious than he'd expected, and his thoughts were going wild. As much as he knew it would anger her, he had to know one other thing. "Have you slept with him?"

She couldn't believe he asked that, and stared at him with daggers in her eyes.

"*That* is none of your business," she spit out, trying to maintain control of her temper.

Actually, Steve felt it *was* his business, and held his ground. "I think it is. You're my sister, and I brought you out here. And you're a Christian."

Britne knew what he was trying to say, and he was right, but she refused to surrender her own right to make those choices.

"That doesn't make my private affairs any of your business, unless I want to tell you. What goes on between Paul and me is between *Paul* and *me*… and *God*." She stood there defiantly, crossing her arms to emphasize her point. "Besides, if I remember correctly, I came out here on my own, against your wishes. Don't worry, Steve, I know what I'm doing."

Steve looked away exacerbated. He was getting nowhere, and turned back to her, speaking from his heart, now.

"Just know this, little sister… you are the most important person in my world. Nobody else matters to me."

"I do know that, and you matter more to me than anyone else," she explained, the edge coming off her voice. "But I'm not a little girl anymore. You've got to let me live my own life, and trust my judgment."

There was no winning this battle—today at least—and Steve knew when to give up. "You're right. I'm sorry."

Britne walked over to the pool table, hopped up to sit next to him, then leaned over and kissed him on the cheek. "That's okay. One of the reasons I love you so much is *because* you try to protect me. Please don't ever stop, and don't ever change. But," she paused, "give me some room, okay?"

"I'll try," he said honestly, not sure how much more room he could give. He looked at his watch, and decided they had done enough cleaning for the day. "We have enough time for a game or two before we open. What do you say?"

"Well, I was going to catch some 'rays,'" she deadpanned, looking out the window at the continuing rain. "But…"

"Rack 'em up, baby!"

THE RAPIDS

This is more like it, Britne thought. She was laying out, sunbathing at "The Rapids," a stretch of about a hundred yards where the tops of giant boulders, whose bodies lay well beneath the floor of the river, danced across the breadth of the tributary, forming rapids comprised of small waterslides and waterfalls. Some of the boulders were large enough to hold a half-dozen people, while others were perfect for just one, and many were clustered so close together that the water swirled around them and formed pools between them where people could swim and relax. It was like the Lord Himself had placed these rocks in precisely the right place to create the most awesome natural water park.

It was sunny and warm today, but the breeze created by the running water around the boulders kept the area cool and comfortable. It was her favorite place in the world to escape to, and was secluded and difficult to find, if you didn't already know the place existed; so, it offered some privacy to a respectful young woman trying to get some sun, away from someone else's ogling eyes.

She looked over at Paul, sprawled out next to her, sound asleep. He'd refused to join her on so many occasions before, but finally gave in to her pouting. Though given far more to convictions than lust, she couldn't help but admire his body, and privately admitted the physical attraction she had for him. She liked being around him, too, and in spite of all that Steve warned her about, things weren't nearly as bad as the picture he painted. Watching him, though, she could see the tension on his face. Even in his sleep, peace continued to elude him. She laid back down, praying for him as she did, barely touching his hand with her own fingers.

***

The illusion, a pool of water floating above the desert floor, formed a translucent, wavy barrier between what was clearly seen, and that which was not; a contrast of refreshing coolness in the midst of extreme heat.

Paul ignored the illusion, though, as he ran forward in urgent desperation, more aware, instead, of the pounding of his heart within his chest. Constricting with every breath, the muscles in his throat began to rob him of much needed oxygen, and the heat emanating from the arid soil caused his lungs to burn like fire. If that wasn't bad enough, the soles of his feet were blistering inside his high-tech running shoes, as each jarring step swallowed yet another cubic inch of sand. The jeans he was wearing impeded every stride he took, slowing his progress forward to what seemed a snail's pace. His red T-shirt was soaked in sweat, as was the bandana covering his head. He continued to push his pace, reaching deep within to find that intestinal fortitude his father so often spoke of as he was growing up. Adorned in black riding gloves, his hands and arms pumped like pistons. The hunting knife in its sheath rattled and slapped his thigh, while the gun holstered to his left side pierced the muscle tissue between his ribs.

Suddenly, his body coiled in pain as a cramp formed in his gut, and he came to an abrupt stop, wheezing and gasping for air. Though in better shape than most men his age, his body was now betraying him.

The mirrored, black-framed sunglasses covered his eyes as they darted back and forth, scanning the blazing surroundings with fatal urgency. The shades also exaggerated the sweat flowing from his forehead. Blood was trickling from his nose and the corner of his mouth. His thoughts were racing out of control, rational and irrational, swirling together in a vortex of panic and fear; yet, he was keenly focused on the single, primary task of getting away. Quickly glancing behind, his gaze locked onto the mass of small figures, warped and distorted by the waves of rising heat, moving in his direction.

Any irrational thoughts he may have entertained were immediately dismissed as the internal drive for self-preservation... to survive... regained control, and he took off once again. No matter how fast he ran, the mass of figures grew larger as they began to close the gap. Outfitted much differently than Paul, they were better suited to their more primitive surroundings, and apparently more prepared for this method of pursuit. Swords brandished and shields ready, they ran in unison... and tired slowly. Paul looked back again to see them closing in on him, and realized just how much out of his element he really was. How is it possible, he thought, that Roman soldiers would be chasing him? Without warning, he tripped and stumbled to the desert surface. Rolling over, he glanced back again to see the Romans bearing down on him. Scrambling to his feet, he lunged forward in a sprint for his life. He could hear the sound of the soldier's armor behind him, and reached even deeper to find the strength to keep going, and then fell again... a bad fall...

✳✳✳

Paul bolted from his sleep to a sitting position, startled and taking a huge gulp of air. He looked around where he was, breathing hard and trying desperately to get his bearings. When he finally got focused on his current surroundings, he noticed Britne laying next to his side, staring at him with her eyes wide open. Clearly, he frightened her.

She let him wake up and get a grip before she talked to him.

"Are you okay?" she asked, tentatively, as his breathing began to return to normal.

"Yeah, just a dream."

"Some dream, to wake you up like that," she told him.

"It was just a *dream*, Brit," he snapped.

Taken aback, she returned the curt tone. "Excuse me! You don't have to bite my head off."

Paul finally had all his wits about him. "I'm sorry. I didn't mean to." He looked off to nowhere in particular and ran his hand through his hair.

Britne watched him for a bit, then sat up and scooted next to him. After a moment, she slipped her arm around his, trying to comfort him, hoping he would open up to her.

"You sure you don't want to talk about it?" she asked, giving him one more chance to reveal his thoughts.

Paul hesitated, then decided to open up and talk to her. "Well, this dream I have. It keeps recurring, over and over and over. It's always the same, me being chased by Roman Soldiers. It's white everywhere, blinding white, and—" He stopped himself short, feeling very insecure about the whole thing, then continued, "you probably think I'm nuts."

"No, I don't," she said warmly, holding him tighter to assure him. "I think you're wonderful."

They seldom ever spoke about her faith in God, but this seemed like a perfect opportunity to open up to him.

"Sometimes the Lord speaks to us with dreams. Maybe He's trying to tell you something." She hoped this would spur him to consider the possibility that God had a plan for him.

Paul's response was lukewarm at best. "Yeah, right."

"Well, He could be," Britne persisted.

Paul put on a somber, philosophical face. "I am but a grain of sand in the desert of life." He couldn't help but laugh. "No, no, I got it. 'Like sands through the hourglass, so are the days—'"

"Stop it," she interrupted, laughing at his quick wit, but socking him in the shoulder, anyway, "I'm serious."

Paul threw his arms up in mock defense. "Okay, okay," he submitted.

They both laughed, and then shared a few seconds of sincere eye contact.

Paul had been trying to find the right time to talk to her about his feelings, and this seemed like the perfect chance.

"Y'know, Brit, I, uh… well… I'd like to say something to you." He was uncomfortable, and paused.

"Yes?"

"Well, I just want you to know…" Again, he stopped short.

"Know what?" she inquired, starting to feel nervous. *Oh God,* she pleaded silently, *don't let him break my heart.*

He looked away from her at first, then turned to her and looked shyly into her eyes. "I, um… I love you, Brit."

"Oh, Paul—" She started to say, but was interrupted.

"Wait, I have to finish saying this… now that I've started."

He paused and took a deep breath.

"I don't know… I feel complete when I'm with you, Brit. Accepted for who I am. I'm not used to feeling that way." He chuckled a bit, then continued. "It's kind of scary, actually, 'cause

I've always been in complete control of my life, and telling you this makes me vulnerable, but I had to tell you how I feel. It's been eating me up inside." He looked deep into her eyes. "I love you, Britne Nicole."

Britne leaned her head on his shoulder. "I love you, too, Paul."

They sat in silence for a bit, enjoying the sounds of the water, basking in the revelation between them, happy just to be together. Right then, all was right with their world, and nothing else really mattered.

The sound of footsteps on the path behind them slowly crept into Paul's consciousness.

"Yo… Paul!"

Paul turned to see Luc on the bank of the river. He had that *urgent* look on his face. One Paul knew all too well, and it said something was definitely *not* right.

"Luc, what's up?"

"Tony's done it again, man. This time it's bad. He hit St. John's hospital."

With a deep sigh, Paul grabbed his shoes and started to put them on, and turned to Britne with a grave and angry tone in his voice.

"If God is so loving, then why does he let this happen?"

"I wish I knew, Paul," she responded, then continued speaking from her heart, "but I do know this… He won't force us to do what's right. That's our choice."

Paul didn't want clichés. "He *could* stop all this, y'know."

Britne continued her thought. "He could, but then our will to choose… our free will… would be taken away. He allows us to make the wrong choices, Paul."

"Still—" Paul persisted.

"God," she interrupted, "isn't killing those people. *Tony* is." Britne was being as patient as she possibly could.

Paul was ready to drop the subject. "Whatever," he said. "I don't know, are we still on for tonight?"

"You bet, and come hungry, too, 'cause it's my special spaghetti."

Paul brightened up at that. "Now I *know* you care." He leaned over and kissed her on the lips. A soft, tender, loving kiss. A long kiss. He backed away and looked into her eyes. "You didn't stop me this time."

"You caught me off guard," she whispered, not attempting to hide that she wanted the kiss. Paul took another long look into her eyes. "I gotta go. See you tonight."

"Bye."

Paul got up and walked toward the riverbank.

Britne was putting on her jacket when there was a big splash, and she turned to see what happened.

"Paul?" She called out.

Sure enough, Paul had slipped off the boulder, and was sitting in the middle of the water. He stood up, soaking wet, and looked from Britne, to Luc, then back to Britne.

"I was hot. I meant to do that."

He climbed out of the water and started off with Luc.

"Paul," Britne called. He stopped and turned around to face her.

"Please be careful."

He looked down at his wet clothes, then up at Britne with open arms. "My middle name, Brit."

"Way to go, Gilligan," Luc said as they walked up the path.

"Shut up!"

ST. JOHN'S

One could easily surmise that this scene was a glimpse into hell itself. Smoke was rising from every corner of the lot; sparks spewing forth from fractured and ruptured electrical lines; people in hospital gowns wandering about with distant looks of shock on their faces; moans, coughing, whimpering, cries for help.

What was once a haven of hope, a place for healing, would now be a terrible memory of hope lost; instead of lives saved and rescued from despair, innocence once again became victim to misguided ideologies of hate and fear.

Steve was nearby when he heard the terrible explosion, when he felt the earth shake, when the debris began to rain down all around him. He quickly made his way over to the hospital and offered his help to the squads of police, ambulances, and fire vehicles arriving at the scene all too late. He had seen death before, but not like this. The once seven-story building was little more than a macabre sculpture of strewn blocks and bent rebar. Broken, bent and twisted bodies, and body parts, lay everywhere. His clothes had become saturated with blood. It made him numb as he took it all in, too numb to even be sick.

He was moving rubble from place to place, searching for the living and the dead, and some twenty feet to his right a fireman was carrying a limp body toward the makeshift triage tent. That's when he heard it. It was barely audible at first, and he cocked his head ever so slightly and closed his eyes, hoping to pinpoint the exact location. He heard it again, a soft moan coming from a pile of rubble only a few feet to the left of where he was standing. The numbness that had overtaken him was replaced with panic, and he went to the pile and knelt down, placing his ear as close as he could to confirm what he had heard. A third time he heard the faint voice, peered down into the wreckage, and sure enough, he could make out a small figure from where the sound was coming from. It was indeed a child, and the panic became unbearable.

"I'm coming," Steve yelled urgently, not softly enough to soothe the child.

"Mommy... mommy."

"I'm here, baby," he said, lifting and tossing stone upon stone into a new pile. "I'm right here." Then he prayed. "Oh, Jesus... please." He tossed another huge chunk of concrete, still trying to encourage the child buried below him, "I'm coming."

The child moaned again, and Steve removed another stone. He could see it was a little girl.

"Hey, I need some help, here," he yelled to a group of rescue workers doing their own excavating off to his right, "I found a little girl... alive!"

"I'll be right there," said one of them, "as soon as possible."

Steve removed the rest of the stones himself, and gently pulled the child out, cradling her in his lap.

"Mommy... Mom..." Her cry was cut off as she broke into a coughing fit, her eyes not opening.

"It's okay, baby... it's okay," Steve said, rocking her as he thought her own mother would.

"It... hurts... Mommy," the girl said deliriously, recognizing him as her mother.

He continued to rock her, gently brushing her hair from her face. "Oh, baby, I know it does." Quietly, he prayed, "Father, please help her."

The girl started coughing violently, and then stopped suddenly, as death ended her pain and suffering.

"Sweetheart? Little girl?"

Steve's tears splashed on her cheeks, but gave her no life. The color of her skin began to change, and, realizing she was gone, he set her body down gently, then got up and walked away, unable to suppress his tears.

He was approached by the med-tech he called to earlier. "Were you the one calling for some help?" he asked.

"Huh... what?"

The med-tech immediately grew impatient. "Get a grip, man. Did you find someone, or what?"

"Oh... uh, yeah. She just died." Steve was almost catatonic with grief and anger.

"Where is she?"

"Over there, where she died... in my arms!"

The med-tech had the good sense to go quickly to where he left her body. Steve watched him, and then turned his gaze upward.

"Lord, I'm sorry," he prayed from deep within himself. "I need your help. I'm... so... angry! Look at this! How could they do this?" He began walking in no particular direction, then stopped in his tracks, overwhelmed with anger.

"How could *you* let them?"

Across the lot from Steve, Luc's Corvette pulled up to what used to be the emergency room entrance. It had barely come to a stop when Paul jumped out and tried to take in the complete devastation of the scene.

"Jesus Christ! I can't believe this," he exclaimed in total shock.

"What's not to believe, man?" Luc replied on the other side of his car, his door shutting ever so slowly.

"You know what I mean, Luc."

"Yeah… I do."

They started making their way through the rubble, aghast at the destruction and death spread throughout. After a bit, they spotted a familiar face at these incidences.

"Hey, there's Billy," Luc informed Paul, quickly making his way over to him. "Yo, Billy!"

"Hey, Luc… Paul," Billy acknowledged, looking up and seeing them.

"Pretty pathetic, wouldn't you say?" Paul understated.

"What?"

"This," Paul pointed out, a little irritated. "What did you think I was talking about?"

Billy had a stream of tobacco spittle leaking out of the corner of his mouth. "Yeah, well… stuff happens." He seemed put out by it all.

"What kind of statement is that?" Luc asked, incredulously.

Billy's accent got thicker, indicating his irritation and need to be assertive. "If you hadn't noticed… this happens a lot these days," he said with sharp sarcasm.

"But it shouldn't!" Paul jumped in. "And you guys don't do a thing. What's up with that, man?"

Steve had walked up behind them, and eagerly joined in the inquisition. "Yeah, Billy," he said. "What's up with that? Tell us, please!"

Billy got right in his face. "Don't come on to me like that, boy."

Steve held his ground, his eyes burning a hole in Billy's, but addressing Paul and Luc. "Better, yet, I'll tell you what's up. Your friend Billy, here, well, he doesn't want to see this kind of thing stop. As a matter of fact, he likes it. He gets off on it."

"Come on, Steve—" Paul said.

Steve cut him off immediately. "No, Paul! It's time to face the music. Ask him. *Ask* him!" He turned on Billy, again. "You man enough to tell the truth, *boy?*"

Billy wasn't at all prepared for Steve's confrontation, and tried to diffuse it with some fake empathy. "I know you're upset, Steve. We all are—"

Steve cut right in, "I'm not an idiot, man. Don't forget... I *know* about you."

Billy spit some tobacco at Steve's feet in defiance. "Oh, do you?"

"What are you talking about, Steve?" Paul asked, his interest piqued.

"Yeah, Steve," Luc agreed, "what are you saying?"

"You guys really don't know, do you?" Steve asked with a steely edge in his voice.

Paul was getting a bit put out himself, and the sarcasm in his voice showed it. "I guess we don't!"

"Billy is pals with your brother. He's part of all this."

Billy didn't flinch at the claim, and responded a bit overconfidently. "That's a mighty powerful accusation, my friend."

Steve had enough of the redneck, and he punched Billy squarely in the nose, causing it to explode in a bloody shower and sending Billy to the ground on his back. Paul and Luc looked at each other, and then at Steve, in astonishment. Since returning, their friend was not prone to outbursts like this.

Billy was writhing in the pain of a possible broken nose, laying on his back, holding his face with both hands.

Steve stepped up to him, leaned down and pointed his finger directly between his eyes. "I'm not your friend. You… and Tony… you're pitiful henchmen of the devil, and you'll live forever in the fire of hell for this. God damn you to hell, Billy!"

He turned and walked away in an angry fit, and Paul and Luc looked at each other, astonished.

"What was that all about?" Paul asked, both to Luc and himself.

"Billy? What's up?" asked Luc, his voice edgy and suspicious.

Billy, still holding his nose, looked in his general direction, but not in the eyes. "It's outta my control, Luc."

Paul looked at both of them quizzically, then ran to catch up to Steve, who just wanted to get away from the horror of the place. Paul caught him quickly, and sought more info.

"Steve, my friend," Paul implored. Steve gave Paul a sharp, sideways glance. "We are still friends, right?" Paul asked, trying to read his body language.

"I would like to believe so," Steve replied evenly.

Paul grabbed Steve's arm firmly but gently, and the two of them stopped right there.

"Then please tell me what all of that was about," Paul demanded.

Steve's reply was even more vague. "You still don't get it, do you? After all these years, you still don't get it. Unbelievable!"

"Get what?" Paul asked, exasperated. "All I see is you getting all pissed off and punching someone out. I'm confused. Is *that* Christianity?"

"I can't believe you, Paul. Like always, you expect me to be perfect."

"Well, not per—"

Steve cut him off mid-sentence. "Just because I embrace Jesus doesn't mean I'm not human. I'm just a simple man, and I struggle with the same faults and temptations as you. We're all the same, man. It's just that I—and others who profess Jesus—can go to God and receive freely from him. Forgiveness, strength, joy—whatever we need."

Paul was visibly perplexed. "What's that have to do with what happened back there?"

"Even Jesus got angry, Paul. He even made a whip, by hand, and used it to rid his Father's temple of the sinners…"

"You're not making any sense," Paul pointed out, getting very irritated.

Steve paused before going on. "Sometimes, Paul, it's all right—even justified—to hate. 'Hate evil,' the Bible says. Tony, his whole group for that matter, what they're doing… *that's evil!*"

"They are crazy—"

Steve cut him off again. "They're *not* crazy. They know exactly what they're doing, and they do it by choice, willfully. Can't you see what's going on here?" he asked, pointing at the hospital. "This… this is all part of Satan's desperate Hail-Mary pass at the end of a game. He's already lost."

The football reference made Paul chuckle. "Satan's *Hail-Mary* pass?"

The light-heartedness made Steve all the more passionate. "Laugh all you can now, because the day will soon be here when laughter will die, and tears will abound." The irony of what he said sunk in immediately, as he looked around at the scene that surrounded them. "Actually, it's already here."

Steve's soapbox religion was really beginning to get on Paul's nerves. After all, he was the one that turned his back on everyone. He could've helped end all this kind of stuff.

"Give me a break, Steve. You might not want to be a part of any of this, but I do. And I am, and I'm trying to stop those tears."

"But you can't, and you won't. All of this must happen!"

"This *doesn't* have to happen," Paul disagreed passionately. "It could all be *stopped* if we choose."

"Choose what, man?" Steve was fit to be tied. "To kill the bad guys? Choose the lesser of two evils, like two wrongs make everything right, the end justifies the means?"

"No, Steve. Choose to defend life, to protect and preserve the gift of life."

"Is that what you call what you do?" Steve asked, laughing in total exasperation. "Preserve life?"

"Someone's got to do it," Paul said, somewhat piously. "Your *God* isn't."

Steve was not to be denied. "What do you think Jesus was all about? Life has *already* been preserved and death has no victory at all! The sooner you realize that, the sooner you can be free of this burden."

"This burden?" Paul asked, very uptight.

"This war, this personal fight of yours with Tony. He's not the real enemy. Satan is. For your own sake, Paul, let go, and be free! I can't say it any simpler than that."

He turned and walked away, leaving Paul standing there

alone. Paul, not used to people leaving him hanging like that, followed Steve in hot pursuit.

"What are you talking about, bro?"

Steve waved him off as he continued to walk away. "Forget it, Paul."

That was all Paul could take. He grabbed Steve by the arm and turned him around sharply. "Y'know, your attitude really sucks."

The look in Steve's eyes was troubling to Paul—desperate, sad, in terrible pain. Steve kept taking a few steps backward, and tripped over something protruding from the mass of rubble. He fell backward, twisting to protect himself on impact. His head made an awful sound as it slammed into some of the rubble underfoot.

Paul went to help him right away, horrified at what had happened. He bent over to help him up. "Oh, man, Steve, I'm sorry!"

Steve sat up and was bleeding from his forehead, with blood oozing over his left eye and the left side of his face. What was worse, though, for both of them, was what they noticed had caused Steve to stumble. It was a small, bloodied hand of a child, sticking out from beneath the rubble. Paul reached out and gently held the fingers of the hand in his own.

"You're right, Paul," Steve muttered, wiping blood from his eye, and trying to hold the seepage at bay. "My attitude does suck. I shouldn't have hit Billy… I shouldn't get so angry."

Paul just stared at the small, broken hand he was holding, his vision now blurred by the tears welling in his eyes.

Steve was now on his knees next to Paul, and reached out to take hold of both Paul's and the child's hands. "Can you blame me, though? Look around you, my friend."

An awkward silence fell between them, both holding the dead child's hand. The tears could no longer be contained by

Paul's eyes, as he gazed blankly at the devastation around them. After a few moments, they let go of the hand, and together, in a more reverent and humble silence, began to dig the child out from the rubble.

FACE THE MUSIC

Paul's motorcycle kept a silent vigil in the driveway of his house, an imposing machine that dared any other mechanized vehicle to cross its path. Yet one car did brave the two-wheeled sentinel. It was Mark's, which pulled in bravely and confidently. Missy got out of the passenger side and walked toward the front door of the house, turning to offer an admiring wave to her beloved. As the GT pulled away, Missy turned and entered the house, grabbing the mail from the box attached to the exterior wall just left of the door.

There was nothing extraordinary about the living room. It had a typical middle class set-up—sofa, love seat, recliner, coffee table, and entertainment center—all of the usual furnishings, including a baby grand piano. On one wall was an American flag with military medals pinned to it. Below that was a picture of a man and a woman, holding hands and smiling as if they were the happiest couple on earth. The man was wearing an Air Force uniform, and was obviously successful, as he had two silver stars on each shoulder.

Missy was looking through the mail, and with the exception of one envelope, set it all on the surface of the piano.

"Paul," she called out.

"I'm in the bathroom."

She walked down the hallway to the bathroom, where Paul

was preparing to shave, his face lathered with shaving cream. He started shaving as they talked.

"Raving mad?" Missy said, laughing.

"Not me," Paul replied, in absolutely no mood to joke around. "But Tony sure is. Did you hear about St. John's?"

"Yeah… it's on all the news. How horrible."

"I can't believe it, Missy," Paul said as he worked the razor around the contours of his face. "The whole building, leveled, over 200 kids dead. Tony is out of control." He finished shaving, and looked deep into his own eyes in the mirror. "When's it gonna stop?"

"There's only one way Tony's going to be stopped," Missy said gravely, understanding in her own heart that the brother she had grown up with had become a beast.

"You're right!" Paul exclaimed, expressing the decision he had already come to in his mind, "and I think it's about time I *faced the music…* and did something about it." He doused his face, grabbed the towel from the counter and walked past her to his bedroom.

"Oh, Paul," she said. "It's not like you to talk this way."

"Today was different, babe. I'm not the same." He came out of his room holding a tie. "I hate these things."

"She must be special if you're dressing up for her. Is it Steve's sister, Britne?"

"Yes it is."

"I've only talked to her a couple of times. She's so pretty, though."

"Yes, she is. And she's special… very special," Paul stammered, handing her the tie. "Can you do this for me?"

Missy threw the letter on his dresser as she took the tie and began to weave end over end for him. "That's the check from the Air Force, by the way. You'd think they'd stop sending paper checks."

Paul's mind was on something else. "I've gotta stop him, Missy. He's rippin' apart this town, the families of friends we grew up with."

"Just be careful. You're the best part of my life."

Paul took her by the hands. "Don't you worry, I'll be all right... Hey, what's this? A ring?"

Missy blushed, then showed it to him. "Yeah, isn't it beautiful? We picked it up the other day."

"That's great, babe. I'm happy for you... both of you." Paul was beaming at her.

"Thanks, that's important to me. We haven't set a date, yet, but we're definitely getting married and having our baby." She gave him the once-over. "You look very handsome, Paul. You should try this more often."

"Whatever you say, sis." He walked into his room and looked in the mirror, liking what he saw, tie or no tie. "You're right, though."

"Don't let it go to your head... I was just being nice."

"Gotta go," he said, fixing his tie. "Thanks for the help. It's perfect." He kissed her on the cheek, then turned to leave. "Love ya."

"I love you ,too," she responded. Then, before he could leave, she called, "Paul?"

He turned back to her. "Yeah, babe?"

"Stay safe... please!"

"Of course," he said chuckling. "See ya later."

"Bye... have fun."

DEAD END ALLEYS

He mounted his stallion, and headed west into the sunset. Paul chose to leave his visor up, allowing the cool twilight air to swirl within his helmet, a refreshing contrast to the heated battle taking place in his mind. So many questions, so few answers. He knew Tony was out of control, and was just as aware that he, himself, was probably the only one that could stop him. Steve's words haunted him, though: killing is killing... all of this must happen... slave to hate... a better way.

What am I doing? he thought. *And why am I doing it? Maybe Brit's right, maybe God's trying to speak to me. All those little children!* The thoughts kept coming, an endless barrage within his mind... and his heart.

As burdened as his heart was becoming, he still knew one thing for sure. Britne! He loved her more than he'd loved any other before. Today was horrific, he pondered, but tonight was going to be special. Maybe, just maybe, this could be the start of a new life. Maybe, just maybe, he had found the woman that would help him *escape* this life. Just maybe.

Paul pulled up to the curb in front of a small flower shop, and the rumble of his motorcycle's engine purred to a stop. Dismounting his steed, he walked to the rear storage box.

"Open."

The top left side of the trunk slid down into the lower section, and he reached in and pulled out his wallet.

"Shut."

The trunk slid back up, closing and locking with an emphatic latching sound. He tested it to be sure anyway. That was his habit. Satisfied the bike was secure, he went into the store.

The clerk behind the counter was building a beautiful bouquet of bright orange and purple flowers in a frosted crystal vase. The smile on her face testified that she enjoyed her job. Looking up from her aromatic creation, she did a double take, and stifled a chuckle as he entered through the door and approached the counter. His helmet was still on, and with a black leather jacket on over the shirt and tie, he looked a little out of sorts. Still, to the pretty, petite, and polished middle-aged clerk, he was quite a handsome man. At least his eyes were.

"May I have a box of chocolate caramels, please?" Paul requested as he picked up a rose from a vase on the counter

The clerk liked his politeness, a contrast to his formal, rough appearance. "Would you like that wrapped... or just beamed up?"

Paul let out a pleasant laugh, happy for the humorous intervention on his thoughts of the evening. "Can you do that?" He asked, more than willing to partake in this sparring of wits. "Wrapped would be nice."

She smiled. "One moment, please."

The clerk walked to the back room behind the counter and Paul glanced at his watch, wondering how long it was going to take. In less than a minute, however, the clerk returned with a wrapped box.

"That was quick," Paul acknowledged.

"It's a common request, so we pre-wrap them."

"Oh, I see."

"Will there be anything else tonight?"

"No thanks. Just the rose and candy. Kind of cliché for a date, eh?"

"She'll love them both. Most of us do."

As the clerk was adding up the bill, two vehicles drove by out front at a good clip. One was the truck Tony had been in at *Damascus Road*, and the other was a beefed-up Hummer, with what looked like a machine gun mounted to its roof. Both were geared up for hunting, and tonight the quarry was human. Shortly after passing the store, the Hummer made a squealing U-turn, appearing to have found its prey.

Back inside the store, Paul was pulling a $20 bill from his wallet. He never used cash anymore, but tonight was different. The nostalgia of doing so made him feel that much more romantic. As he was handing it to the clerk, he heard the squeal of the tires and turned to see the Hummer whip it's tail end around and head back in his direction. His instincts kicked in without hesitation.

"Keep the change," he told the clerk, who was unaware of the turn of events. From the look on her face, she wasn't used to handling cash, either. He grabbed the candy and turned to run out, stuffing the box and the rose inside his jacket hastily.

"On… Arm… Shields."

When Paul bolted through the door, the motorcycle was already running. Clear Plexiglas shields slid down from the sides and rear of his trunk to cover the tires, up from the front of his trunk to protect his back, and up from the front of the bike to protect his face and chest. Additionally, small cannon-like barrels jutted out from small openings in the rear of both saddle-bags, and another barrel jutted out from under the headlight.

At the same time, Tony and his two companions in the truck were watching the Hummer pull its U-turn as they zipped by it.

"What are they doing?" the driver asked.

"Who knows anymore," a third passenger said. "They're always—"

"Look!" Tony yelled, spotting Paul jump on his motorcycle in front of the store. "There's Paul."

"Where?" asked the driver.

"Comin' out of that store, you idiot. Turn around." Tony was irritated by the inattention of his friends, but was ecstatic, nonetheless, that they had found their nemesis.

The truck pulled a squealing U-turn of its own, and as it did, Paul was taking off from the store, just in front of the Hummer. One of the guys in the Hummer stood up and began to fire the electro-pulse machine gun at Paul. The bolts of electricity could be seen bouncing off the shields and ricocheting in all directions, the sound of windows breaking everywhere from the stray shots.

From Paul's perspective, things were happening fast, but he remained calm, trusting his equipment and experience to get him out of the danger.

"Rear arm." After a second, "LOCKED" was projected on the right corner of his visor, and a warbling tone sounded in the helmet's earpiece, indicating the guns on the rear of his bike had found a target and locked in on it.

"Fire."

On command, an electro-pulse shot out from both barrels in the back of the bike, and hit the Hummer dead-center on the front grill, causing its engine to explode with a mighty roar.

It locked up, skidded around, and launched into a fiery roll, as Paul watched it all in his rear view mirrors with indifference and adrenaline-filled alertness.

Tony saw the guns find their target and the tragic results of it. "Look out!" he yelled with panic in his voice.

The driver reacted with the same kind of panic and fear, veering the Dodge Ram sharply to its left, lifting the two left tires a good foot off the ground as it sped by the flipping Hummer with only inches to spare. With a quick turn back to the right, the tires bounced down onto the ground, and the truck found its center of gravity just in time to grip the road and continue the hot pursuit of Paul on his bike.

"What's he got on that thing?" the driver yelled with a mixture of relief and amazement.

"More than you'll believe," Tony responded, knowing full well his older brother's fascination with high-tech gadgetry.

A fleeting memory of himself standing outside their home as a child, watching Paul and his dad drive off, crossed his mind. They were off to Quantico, VA, where Paul would have the privilege of touring one of the government's secret weapons labs. He remembered crying as he stood there, wanting so desperately to go with them, but unable to because he was too young. He wasn't that much younger than Paul, but then again, he wasn't his dad's favorite, either.

Returning to reality in a split second, his jealousy of Paul was even stronger. He snapped at the driver, "Can you shield your engine?" He wanted no part of the guns on Paul's motorcycle.

"What, are you kidding?" The driver exclaimed. "That stuff costs big bucks."

Tony rolled his eyes. "Then what *do* you have?"

"Charm, good looks, and a big—"

"Ego!" Tony interrupted, finishing the sentence for him. "That's just great."

"There's a 'Twin' under the seat," offered the passenger, reaching down and pulling a short, stocky, double-barreled hand-held machine gun from beneath their legs.

Tony perked up some, glad to have something he could use to keep his brother off balance. "Now we're talkin'! Hand it here."

He grabbed the 'Twin,' and started to climb over the passenger, who was sitting next to the door. "Hold my legs," he demanded, wrapping the gun strap around his right arm a couple of times.

It was times like this Paul wished he had chosen one of those perky, high-acceleration speed bikes. He really loved the power of his beast, but he sure wished he had a bit more pick-me-up right now. Still, he was grateful for the loyalty that his father had developed amongst his subordinates and peers; there was no way he could possibly have tricked out his motorcycle the way he had without the goodwill, and under-the-table generosity, of his dad's old connections. Paul was now using every defense the motorcycle had to shake off the truck.

"Slick."

Oil and grease spilled out from the bottom of his saddlebags, forming a slick spot at least twenty feet across and a hundred feet long.

There was no way for the truck to avoid it and it spun in a full 360-degree circle to the left, twice. Tony's driver was up to the task, and never seemed to lose a beat as he cranked the steering wheel hard to the right and straightened the Ram back up, the rear end swerving a bit but staying on track.

Tony had been climbing out the passenger window when they hit the slick spot, and was out as far as his waist. Holding on for dear life, his left hand was gripping the frame of the window. Once the driver cranked hard right to straighten the truck up, the door he was leaning out flew open, taking him with it. At high velocity, it pounded the side of the front end just over the tire and, still gripping the door frame, the side of his face slammed into the hood of the truck. The door bounced off the side and headed back to its intended position. This forced Tony's body to shoot downward, still gripping the window with his lift hand, bringing his head level with the bottom of the door. His legs flipped upward, a natural counterweight to the downward thrust of his upper body. This actually saved him, because they wrapped around the top of the window frame like a monkey's tail on a tree branch. Tony's forehead hit the running board along the bottom of the vehicle, which kept the door from slamming shut and crushing his shin bones.

The other passenger reached out in horror, grabbed Tony's legs, and pulled him in as fast as he could. Once he was somewhat secure in the truck, Tony threw two quick jabs with the butt of the 'Twin' to the head of his incompetent partner.

"I told you to hold my feet," he screamed in frightful relief, "you freakin' idiot." He wiped some blood off his forehead, and was ready to take matters into his own hands. "Now, hold me, tight," he told the passenger. He leaned out of the window again and fired the 'Twin,' barely able to keep the aim on Paul and keep himself in the truck. Electro-bursts flooded the night air, bouncing off the rear shields of the motorcycle in an awesome display of fireworks. All but one, that is, which skimmed by the shield, ripping a huge gash across the top of Paul's left hand.

"Ah, Jesus Christ," he yelped in pain, and instinctively put the motorcycle on auto-pilot. "Auto, on." His trusted mount took over, but at the expense of the evasive maneuvering Paul was capable of.

"You hit him, Tony. Great shot!" the passenger exclaimed with excitement, sharing a high-five with the driver.

Tony, climbed into the cab and brought them back to earth. "Save the praise and stow the party. Just catch him!"

"I'm tryin', man," the driver rebutted in defense, "but he's still goin'. He's good."

"He's good as dead if you just catch him," Tony screamed in utter disdain.

Just ahead, Paul was formulating a plan, a way of getting out of this mess. After all, he had a dinner date with his dream girl, and she was making her special spaghetti. There was no way he was going to miss that.

"Go right!" he commanded, and the motorcycle submitted to his words, slowed down, leaned to the right, and zipped up a road lined with trimmed lawns and shaped hedges.

The driver of the Dodge didn't react quickly enough, and passed by the street Paul had just turned on. He slammed his brakes, ripped the steering wheel to the left, and forced the vehicle into a 270-degree about-face. With pedal to the metal, the tires spun at ten times their normal rotation, filling the air with gray smoke that stunk of burned rubber. He then maneuvered his truck onto the avenue Paul was using as his escape. The street was a winding path with minimal lighting, and Paul was nowhere to be seen.

Looking over his shoulder, Paul could see he had given himself some time and space, and intended to make full use of this advantage. At least, that was his plan.

"Go right!"

The motorcycle once again obeyed his command, and headed up an even darker boulevard that looked like it, too, had enough bends in it to offer Paul even greater freedom from his pursuers.

In the truck, they had slowed down and were passing the turn Paul had just made.

"We lost him," Tony spewed out with vitriol. "I can't believe that; he's freakin' hurt, and still gets away."

"Chill out, Tony," said the driver.

Tony reached across the seat, grabbed the driver by the hair on the back of his head and smashed his face into the steering wheel twice, causing the horn to blow each time. Pointing his finger, he let loose on the driver, "If you could drive we'd have had his sorry—"

Just then, Paul hauled by, as his expected escape route intersected the road he thought he had left behind.

"There he goes!" yelled the passenger.

Tony smacked the driver on the side of his face with the back of his hand. "Now's your chance for redemption," he said, watching Paul drive ahead on his motorcycle. "Get it together, man… let's go!"

The driver, still dazed and bleeding from his nose, floored the gas pedal and peeled around the turn after Paul, who still had a decent cushion between the pickup and himself.

Paul had noticed the truck on his left when he crossed the intersection. Looking over his shoulder, he figured that he could still break free from them. Turning back to look ahead, his heart seemed to stop as he realized with dread and despair that the street led directly to a dead end, and it was closing in fast.

"Son of a… Brake!"

The bike came to a quick stop, just at the end of the street, and Paul looked over his shoulder once more to see the headlights of his tracker's vehicle drawing ever closer. Right away his thoughts flashed back to his conversation with Luc not too long ago.

"Well, Luc, you're right again," Paul said to himself. He climbed off and pulled his rifle from the right side holster.

"Off, lock, secure."

The motorcycle shutdown automatically; the lights, mirrors and everything in the front faring slid into protective covers; all the shields slid back into place, the tires deflated, and an arrow-like bar shot down into the street from the left-side saddlebag, anchoring the vehicle into place. This machine was going nowhere.

Paul stood in front of his motorcycle as the truck came to a slow stop about ten yards from him. All three guys got out, Tony with the 'Twin,' the passenger holding a steel pipe, and the driver empty handed. The faces of all three were bloodied, and Paul couldn't help but laugh to himself at the sight of the men. They casually approached so that Tony stood directly in front of him, the passenger to his left, and the driver to his right, arms folded in confidence.

Tony was chuckling in a sinister kind of way as he inched even closer to his brother.

"Looks like the fox is cornered, guys. Tell me, Paul, how's it feel?"

Paul had been in worse situations than this before, and was incredibly calm as Tony came closer. "Hopeless… maybe."

Paul suddenly did a half-turn to his left, and planted his

right foot in the stomach of the passenger. Completing the turn full circle, he swung the butt of his rifle in an upward arch, contacting the left side of the man's face, snapping his head to the right and lifting him off the ground in a twisting motion. Before the man hit the ground, Paul rolled head-over-heels in the other direction. With the agility of a trained operative, he leapt back to his feet, took two quick steps across the divide, and smashed the butt of his rifle into the driver's forehead, sending him crumbling to the ground as well. Completing his trifecta, in one fell swoop, he spun to his right, made a swing with his rifle that knocked the 'Twin' out of Tony's hands, and finished up holding the muzzle of the rifle to Tony's throat.

"On the other hand," he whispered in Tony's ear, "there's *always* hope!"

The sound of an explosion filled his head, as something smashed down onto his helmet, causing him to drop his rifle unexpectedly. Reacting with split second decisiveness, he lifted his right knee to Tony's gut with enough force to lift him in the air and drop him to the ground. He spun on his heels to see that the passenger had pickup up the pipe again, and was now shifting his eye contact back and forth between Paul and the pipe. The stunned look on his face was classic, and Paul quickly kicked him in the groin.

"Better than Motrin," he quipped, tapping his helmet. The passenger held his groin with a beet-red squint on his face, and fell to the ground writhing in pain, unable to even utter a moan.

Seizing the opportunity, Paul picked up his rifle, hurdled over Tony, and took off running past the truck.

Tony pulled himself off the ground and started after Paul, not many steps behind his brother. With a leaping lunge, he hurtled himself through the air and locked his right arm around Paul's neck, at the same time knocking the rifle from Paul's hand with his left arm. They continued forward another five or so steps, Tony trying frantically to drag his brother to the ground, before coming to a stop. Tony thought that he had Paul for sure, forgetting just how resourceful he could be.

Paul was having trouble breathing, as Tony's arm was wrapped tightly around his neck and throat. He reached back with his right hand, put Tony's groin into a vice grip, and heard a loud grunt. The arm around his neck quickly loosened, enough for him to slam his helmet backward into Tony's face twice.

Tony melted to the ground and laid there, his nose and mouth awash in blood.

Paul slowly removed his helmet, turned around to face Tony, and casually stepped over him to be able to look into his face. Exhausted and breathing hard, he removed his pistol from its holster and pointed it at his brother.

Tony was laying there on his side in tremendous pain. Looking up at Paul, he snarled like the cornered animal he was, literally bearing his teeth at Paul and the gun pointing at his head. "Go ahead... do it!"

"Shut up!" Paul responded.

Tony laughed a dark, evil laugh from deep within his bowels. "You don't have it in you to do me, Paul."

Then and there, images and pictures filled Paul's mind... the two of them as kids, running toward the stack of mattresses, bouncing off the bottom one, hurtling themselves five feet above their heads to the very top mattress, bounding to their feet and wrestling over who was the "mattress diving champ"... Tony always tagging along with his band, begging just to help set up his drums... the one-on-one basketball games in their back yard that always inevitably turned into "tackle" basketball...

Paul smiled at him serenely, knowing he held the upper hand at the moment. "Oh, I've got it in me. I'm just not gonna give in to it. I still love you, man. I hate what you do, but I still love you."

Tony was still gasping for air, and looked deep into Paul's eyes, unfazed by the words of compassion just spoken. "You're such a fool, fightin' a lost cause."

Paul was suddenly overcome with sadness and pity. "I don't understand you, Tony. What happened? You were never like this growing up."

"Spare me the big brother talk, Paul. I stopped carin' what you thought years ago."

"But why?" Paul asked, needing to understand. "Why kill so many innocent people? All those children?"

"It's my *job*, man," Tony said, with all the sarcasm he could muster.

"Your job?" Paul asked with an unbelieving chuckle. "You and the devil," he continued sarcastically, staring down at his brother in amazement. He was totally unprepared for Tony's response.

Letting out that cold, hollow, evil laugh once again, Tony looked straight into Paul's eyes. "You're just figuring that out? Jesus, Paul, everything I do has a purpose. The churches, schools, synagogues... everything... Call me the devil's advocate." He looked proud of his work.

"You're pathetic, Tony." Paul was getting a little ticked off at this point. "You mock everything that Pop lived—"

Tony cut him off right there. "Our father was hung dead doing his duty for God and Country. Well, I hate them both, and I'm doing everything I can to destroy them." He chuckled at that. "Y'know, it's funny. Luc basically said the same thing... just before I snuffed him, that is." He was laughing out loud now.

Paul was overcome with rage, and readied himself to shoot Tony right between the eyes. "He's my best friend!"

"He's your dead friend, now," Tony said, unabashed and mockingly.

The look on Paul's face was sheer rage. He had always thought it might end this way, his own hand being the one to swing the hammer and bring an end to Tony's insanity. He hadn't figured it might come at the price of his best friend's life. His thoughts weren't racing, though; rather, they were calm and calculating in the midst of his cold sweat and pounding heart. He was ready! Now was the time to end all this terror. He could do it now! He was ready... to kill Tony, and feel no remorse, because it had to be done. He was ready, and began to pull back on the trigger with his finger.

Then, suddenly, he wasn't. He *wasn't* ready. He was confused. More childhood memories, followed by images of the children's bodies at the hospital. He imagined how it must have been for Luc. Was it painful, or quick? *Oh God,* he cried out in his heart. Then, looking into Tony's eyes one more time, he saw something different. A pleading, begging, wanting look. *I have to do this,* Paul thought to himself. *It has to be done.* But he just couldn't bring himself to pull the trigger. Was it compassion? No, he rationalized. Was it cowardice? Certainly not, because he feared nothing. Was it the simple fact that he didn't want to give Tony the satisfaction of a quick death? Was it all of the above? Or none of the above? All this process lasted but a few seconds, and in the end, he slowly lowered his gun to his side and just stared at Tony.

And Tony stared back, pursing his lips, wishing that the trigger had been pulled.

Without warning, the butt of a rifle came crashing down on Paul's head. He crumpled to the ground, folding like a marionette without strings. Paul had let his guard down, forgetting about the other two guys… and one of them didn't hesitate to remind him they were there.

Tony cackled with delight at the fine work of his henchman. The driver helped Tony to his feet, and the three of them looked at Paul laying there on the ground. Then they celebrated… by playing hacky-sack with Paul's body, kicking him over, and over, and over. For nearly a minute this went on, until they grew bored with it and sought out more compelling things to do with their time. They turned and began to walk back toward their truck.

Then Tony stopped and turned around. Tipping an imaginary hat, he nodded his head and closed his eyes. Then he opened them slowly, and took one last look at his brother's limp body.

BRUISED AND BROKEN

Standing at the counter, Britne glanced over her shoulder, being fit to be tied, and noticed the clock on the wall above the kitchen table read 10:32. She looked at the table, set for two in her best wares. A candle still flickered in the middle, but had melted nearly to the bottom, with wax leaking onto the tablecloth.

Soft jazz was playing on the stereo, as she opened a can of cat food and put it on a plate. At her feet, to the right of the counter, her cat was purring in delight as it nibbled away at her bowl, filled with the cold spaghetti from her lovingly prepared meal.

"You like that, Whisper, sweetie?" She asked her cat rhetorically. "Good for nothing," she continued to herself. "Oh, he's bound to be hungry!" Reaching above her to the right, she pulled out another can of cat food, and sarcasm overcame her. "The girl of my dreams, my dream come true… yeah, right!"

There were some belabored knocks at her door. Grabbing the plate with the cat food, she turned toward the door, dropping the plate on the table as she went by. She looked at the setting once again. "Perfect," she said to herself, then headed for the door. "Stay in control now," she muttered as she reached for the handle. Swinging open the door, she began her diatribe before he had a chance to say a word. "If you think that—"

She gasped in mid-sentence, completely unprepared for what stood before her eyes. There he was, leaning against the door frame, bruised and battered, dry blood caked all over his face and neck. His clothes were torn and tattered. If there was any modicum of decency, it was the manner in which he held out the gifts he had purchased for her. With his eyes closed, and his head flush against the door frame, he held a broken, smashed rose and a crushed box wrapped in shredded rose-filled wrapping paper in his right hand, close to his body. His helmet was in his left hand, dangling as his arm hung limply by his side.

"Hi there," he said, with a smile trying to make its way through the pain he was in. He held up her gifts. "I got these… just for you."

Britne turned white at the sight of him, and panic filled her voice. "Oh my goodness… what happened?"

"I sort of got mugged." He made himself laugh, but it hurt every bone in his body to do so. "You should see the other guy, though."

"Oh, Paul, come in." She took him by the arm and he winced with pain. "I'm sorry."

"That's okay. It only hurts if I laugh."

She guided him to the table. "Here, sit down," she said, looking at this man she loved, so broken, as he gingerly sat down. "I'll be right back."

He sat at the table and leaned back against the wall, as she ran to the back of her apartment. She came back with the usual first aid items—peroxide, towels, cotton balls and swabs. She put peroxide on a cotton swab, and touched the wounds on his face with it. Just the slightest touch caused Paul great pain.

"Ow! Be gentle with me," he exhaled with labored speech, turning his head to his left. Spotting the cat food on the table, he couldn't help but make light of the situation. "Looks like I missed a good one," he whispered jokingly, then realized just how upset Britne must have been. "I'm sorry for missing dinner."

"Stop," she rebuked with tenderness and concern, "don't be sorry." She was trying hard to contain herself, and guilt for the anger she had felt flooded her heart. "You almost got yourself killed. What happened to you?" She was doing the best she could, tending to his wounds with hands that were shaking.

"Yeah, well, I ran into Tony at the store," he explained, and then remembered the items he was holding, "Oh, these are for you." He handed her the remnants of his romantic gift.

"Oh, Paul. We've got to get you cleaned up. Let's go over to the couch."

She stood to her feet, and tried to get him to stand as well, but he was very slow to respond.

"Come on."

Gingerly, he stood up with her help. Sitting at the table had helped release some of the adrenaline, and his body began to tighten up and become very sore. "Okay, but like I said, be gentle. I'm fragile." He smiled through at all, though, finding great comfort just being in Britne's company.

Walking to the couch in the center of the living room, he noticed two small stone tablets of the Ten Commandments, just like the ones at the club, sitting atop a faux mantel against the wall to his right. Next to the tablets was a picture of a dark-haired guy, wearing a T-shirt that had the word "FAITHWALK" on the front.

Britne helped him sit on the couch, and he leaned back and closed his eyes, finally feeling some semblance of comfort.

To Britne, though, he looked in terrible pain, and it seemed his condition was worsening. "I'll be right back, don't move," she commanded, the worry in her voice quite evident.

Paul's moan was his only response, as Britne dashed to her restroom, again, to find some more first aide items. She was rummaging through her cabinets in a frenzy, when she stopped and just stared into the mirror for a moment, tears running down her cheeks. She pulled herself together, gathered all that she could find, and headed back into the living room.

Setting herself down next to him, she attended to the myriad of cuts, scrapes, gashes and bruises that were all over his face, neck, chest and back. It was a slow process. She wasn't prepared to do this kind of thing, but as she was finishing up, he appeared to look much more like a human being again. His face had been cleaned, and she was treating the wounds on his back.

"I'm almost done, here. A couple more spots—"

"Ahhhhhh!" He interrupted, as she dabbed some peroxide on another wound. He didn't know which was worse, the beating or the cleaning. She quickly tended another scrape. "Ahhhh!"

"And I'll be finished," she continued, not quite satisfied she had treated everything.

"You enjoy this, don't you?" He jokingly asked her, looking over his shoulder. "It makes you... *Ow!*... feel powerful."

"There, all done."

It took every effort to get his T-shirt back on, and she had to help him get it over his head as carefully as possible. He turned his body to sit on the couch a bit more comfortably, and looked over at the amazing woman sitting next to him.

She looked into his eyes with tremendous concern. "You really need to go see a doctor."

"I'll be fine," he said matter-of-factly. Then, with the most sincerity, he offered, "Thanks."

"Sure… Y'know, I never understood what Steve was running from until you walked through that door, tonight."

"I didn't either… but I saw some things today that really disturbed me."

"You mean it never bothered you before?"

He thought back to the hospital. "Sure it did, but today was different. When I was at the hospital today, pulling those kids' bodies from the rubble, I wanted to kill my brother. I mean, I really hated him."

"Your brother?"

"Yeah, Tony. You didn't know that?"

"No."

"I thought Steve might have told you."

Paul always had difficulty talking about his former comrade-in-arms, but with Britne it was worse. Like those times, as a kid, when he cussed, and his mom would put shampoo all over his tongue, and then make him swish water around his mouth. Yes, talking with her about Steve was difficult.

Britne, for her part, became irritated at the mere mention of her brother's name. "The only time Steve talks about you is when he's telling me how wrong you are for me."

Paul chuckled at that, wincing a bit at the pain it caused. "That figures. But he's right, y'know."

"He just thinks I'm going to get hurt, somehow. He worries." She was close to tears.

"I would, too, if you were my sister," Paul agreed. "I'd never hurt you, though, Brit. You know that, right?" She nodded. "I've dreamt of meeting you all my life." He looked up to see the sadness in her face. "What's wrong?"

A tear finally made its way down her cheek. "Why do you keep saying that… 'the girl of my dreams'?"

He looked deep in her eyes. "Because it's true, it's how I feel. Does that bother you?"

"A little," she admitted, hesitantly.

"Why?" He was bothered that this would cause her pain, and didn't understand it at all.

"I don't know, Paul. It just sounds too much like cheap flattery."

Her words hurt, and he began to struggle with what was happening right now. After all he'd just gone through, this was the last thing he needed to be hearing.

"I'm sorry you feel that way, 'cause I don't mean it like that."

Britne sensed his disappointment, and tried to backtrack. "I'm sorry, I shouldn't have said anything."

"No, I'm glad you did." He was trying to be as understanding as possible, and, although he failed to see her point of view, put forth his best effort not to get upset at all this. "I think I understand."

After the most uncomfortable silence, Britne finally asked, "You thirsty?"

"Sure."

Britne got up and walked to the kitchen, while Paul got up, very carefully, and walked to the mantel to look at the picture he noticed earlier.

"Mountain Dew, Iced tea, O.J?" she asked from the kitchen.

"I'll take a Dew," Paul said.

Grabbing a couple of sodas from the fridge, she walked back

into the living room, and noticed Paul looking intently at the picture. She joined him at the mantel.

"He was a family friend. His name was Trip."

A sad realization hit Paul.

"Was?"

"Another undeserved victim of this God-awful killing," she answered, a bit reserved.

"I'm sorry," he offered, taking an even closer look at the picture. The two "A" letters in the word "FAITHWALK" on his shirt were formed by two legs in a walking motion, and the 'T' was a cross.

"What's this on his shirt… Faithwalk?"

"He walked across the country, from New York to Mexico." Her voice was hollow.

Paul was incredulous. "Why would anyone in their right mind do something like that?"

She pointed to the stone tablets with the Ten Commandments.

"For those."

Paul was perplexed. "I don't get it."

Britne explained it to him patiently.

"He walked across the country, to bring attention to our need, as a culture and a nation, to turn back to God's commandments. He would tell anyone who listened that without them, society would degrade into anarchy. I guess he was right. He gave his life… trying to share that truth."

"I'm sorry to hear that," he said after a reverent pause. Noticing a book on the mantel, as well, he picked it up. The title read, *"The Ten Words That Will Change A Nation."*

"Is this his, too?" he asked.

"Yes," she answered, a bit melancholy. "He wrote it about the Ten Commandments. It's a great book."

Paul was more than ready to get off the subject. He walked back to the couch and sat down, letting out a heavy sigh. Britne followed him and sat down beside him, bringing her right leg under her left.

"Can I ask you something?" she inquired, turning to face him.

"Shoot!" he said, quickly catching the irony of that statement and making light of it. "Not literally, though."

She smiled at his humor, but continued directly. "I was wondering... well... why do you do what you do?"

"What, with Tony?"

"Yes."

"It's not easy to explain," he said, taking a deep sigh before continuing. "My dad was a high military attaché to the Middle East during the early years of the 'Terror Wars.' When Iran hit Tel Aviv with their first nuclear missile, it served as a catalyst for the radical Islamic coups in other counties like Lebanon, Iraq, Qatar... but the biggie was Saudi Arabia, where my parents were living at the time. When the fundamentalists wiped out the royal family, the government collapsed. They had all Americans executed as spies. Both my parents were hung in public, as an example."

"Oh, Paul... I'm sorry... that's terrible. It must have been hard."

Paul continued, glad to share this with her. "It was, actually. Tony and I had already moved out, but Missy was still living at home. When dad was being transferred, the two of us agreed to move back home to take care of her while they were gone. We didn't mind, actually, 'cause we all got along great. When they

Damascus Road

were killed, it freaked us out. After a while, Tony just split. We didn't hear from him for years. So, it was Missy and me. Between my folks insurance, and my dad's Air Force retirement, we survived. We kept the house, which we grew up in, and still live there today. But, it was hard... emotionally... you know what I mean?"

Britne understood all too well. It was much the same for her, but instead of having her brother with her, she had lived through the loss of her own parents feeling alone and isolated.

"Yeah, I had the same problem. So, where did Tony go?"

"I have no idea," Paul continued. "Like I said, he didn't keep in touch. I didn't even know he was home until some of the gang spotted him; and when we tied him to these attacks, it blew my mind."

The guilt that he'd struggled with was coming to the surface.

"I felt responsible. My dad would have expected me to keep us all together, somehow. I let him down, though, and my brother has turned out the way he is."

"You can't blame yourself—"

Paul quickly disagreed. "I could have done something to make all this different."

"Like what?"

Paul was getting irritable. "I don't know. Something."

Britne couldn't let this kind of talk continue. She could see that it was eating him up inside.

"Listen, Paul. You can't bash yourself over the head because of Tony." The words came out before she caught herself.

"He did a good job of that himself, tonight," he joked again.

This time, Britne's guilt for being so insensitive and stupid kept her from appreciating his good-natured sense of humor.

"You know what I mean. He's made his own choices. Choices of the heart, and soul. That's between him and God."

"No, no."

He got up a little too quickly, and winced at the sharp jabs of pain that coursed through his body, which wasn't at all appreciative. Still, his emotions were getting the best of him, and he continued.

"Can't you see. This is between him and me, and he knows it. What he's doing is wrong. He knows that, too, but he rubs it in my face. It's like he's saying that my whole life, and my dad's life, is nothing but a joke."

Britne was steadfast, trying the best she could to help him see the real truth in all this.

"They *all* know, Paul; everyone who's a part of this terrorism. They know exactly what they're doing, and they've chosen that path for themselves." She got up and walked over to him. "Just like you've chosen yours, and I've chosen mine. We all make our own choices, and we'll have to account for them one day."

"Yeah," Paul said, taking a deep breath and trying to get a handle on his feelings, "but it's hard to make the right choice, anymore, with nothing but death, murder, hate… everywhere."

"I can only speak for myself," Britne said with conviction, "but I choose to love. Love is the only thing that can conquer hate."

She had a thought, and figured out how she might be able to get him to understand. "Hold on a sec," she said, and walked to the back of her apartment, to her room. "Can you come here, please?"

He walked to her room, unsure of what to expect, but anticipating that he had trouble hiding.

"Yes?"

She patted the bed next to her. "Come sit next to me, please. I want you to read something." She was holding a Bible.

"Aw, Brit, I don't want to read that," he said, sounding more disappointed than he would have liked to.

"Please," she pleaded, with the look of a sad puppy. "For me?"

"Okay, okay."

He surrendered to the natural power that women like Britne held over men like him, walked over to the bed and sat down next to her.

She handed him her Bible, and he grudgingly took it from her.

"I never could say no to baby blues like yours." With a deep, submissive sigh, he asked, "Where do I start?"

She pointed to the verses. "Here, and stop here."

Paul sighed once again, then began reading the passage at breakneck speed, like he was trying to recite something from memory before he could forget the words.

"Love is patient, love is kind—"

Britne, being the feisty, independent young lady she was, socked him good and hard in the shoulder, forgetting for just a moment the pain his body was currently suffering.

"Slow down."

"Ow!" Paul whined.

"You really are a baby, sometimes," she said, irritably.

"All right, all right," he surrendered, laughing, which brought even more pain.

Continuing, he read the verses she pointed out, "Love is patient, love is kind; Love is not envious, or boastful, or proud. Love is not rude, or selfish, or quick to anger. Love keeps no record of wrongs, hates evil…" He paused momentarily at that, recalling Steve's argument at the hospital, then continued, "and rejoices in truth. Love always protects, always hopes, always trusts, and always perseveres. Love never fails." He paused again, staring at the words for a couple of seconds, not quite sure what to make of them. "There, I've read it."

"Did you get it's meaning?"

"Why?"

"Because, Paul... *that's* what real love is. Hope, trust, patience, kindness. If we all lived according to that principle, then the world would be very different. But, we all don't, so the world is what it is. One by one, though, if we all choose to love, then maybe... maybe... we can make some changes for the better."

Paul's attention to what Britne was saying had already been lost. Not since that first night at the club had his senses been so stimulated by her smell, her voice, her eyes... her form. His mind kept wandering to things less spiritual, and much less wholesome. In all the time they spent together, seldom had they been so *close* to each other. She was very good at keeping a certain distance between them. Sitting here now, in such close proximity, his body was speaking to him in ways that were difficult to contain. Obviously she cared for him, and her heart was troubled by how near death he had come. He wanted to let her know *exactly* how he felt, and all this talking only embedded deeper into his heart just how much he loved her. Even as she was speaking of this love from the Bible, he couldn't stop *looking* at her... how her lips moved, the arch of an eyebrow, or the gleam in her eyes as she spoke so passionately.

"You know, Brit," he said softly, tenderly, as he leaned in toward her, a look of passion in his own eyes, "all this talk of love..."

She looked at him as he began to speak, and something was different. There was a deeper longing in his eyes tonight, a genuine tenderness that made her want to wrap her arms around him and just hold him. Slowly, she backed away when he began to move in closer, and in doing so found herself laying on the bed with Paul above her, looking down at her. She could feel her heartbeat quicken, and her breathing had changed.

She began to think it might not have been such a good idea to have called him to her room. If he hadn't shown up in the condition he was in, it would've been much easier to keep him at arms length. If not for his condition, she wouldn't have even let him in the door at that late hour.

No matter, she couldn't hide from the feelings she had for him, or from her desire for him. For a couple of months, now, she had thought about the possibility of being in this kind of situation, but it was easier to deal with the myriad of imagined scenarios when they were just fanciful thoughts. Now, it was much more difficult. Her breathing was becoming erratic, and though she knew she *wanted* this to be happening… she also knew, without a doubt, that she *didn't*.

"Your dinner's getting cold, Paul."

"How about we… skip dinner," he said, kissing her on the lips tenderly, tentatively, "and just have dessert." He kissed her again. A long, soft, deep kiss. And then he continued kissing her, down to her neck. His hands began exploring. His breathing changed to a shorter, fireier tempo.

This was a little more than Britne was comfortable with. But it felt so good, and she didn't know what to do. She didn't want this moment to stop. Her body was waking up to the feelings that had been laying in wait for months, luring her to this place where they could escape their prison. But her heart was crying out as well. She had lived her life devoted to her faith... to her Lord... and had committed her heart, her mind, her soul and her body to the purity of that relationship. No man could have that part of her until the time that was set aside for them. And definitely *not* like this. She eased her hands to his chest, torn between the desires of her flesh, and the passion of her heart.

"Paul," she whispered into his ear, drawing on the strength of her faith to push against his chest, "this... this isn't right."

At first, Paul didn't understand what she was saying, but she kept pushing against him... pushing him away. Slowly, hesitantly, he stopped and pulled his head back so he could look down into her eyes. He saw in those eyes the same wanting that was in his heart. Then, he saw the fear. It confused him terribly, and he kept looking into her eyes. And it was very clear what they were saying to him.

Stop. Please stop.

"What's not right?" he asked her plaintively, hoping she would answer back with an equal submission to the desires he *knew* they both had. Instead, she gave him silence, and eyes that wouldn't keep contact with his.

"I love you, Brit. You make me feel like I've never felt before in my life. Everything around us... just melts away when I'm around you. You're all I've ever wanted... and I think you feel the same way, too."

Britne's reply was cautious. "Maybe."

"Maybe?" Paul was incredulous. This didn't make any sense to him. She had said she loved him many times. She was confusing him without end. "*Maybe!?*"

"Yes, I do," she said softly, "but..."

Britne stopped short, and her hesitation was more than obvious.

"But, what?" By now, Paul had lost the passion of the moment, and was becoming irritated. Angry. Hurt.

Britne looked away, fighting back tears. "You won't understand."

Paul was really struggling now to maintain his composure. "I fell in love with you the moment I first laid eyes on you. I knew it then, and I know it now. I just want to share that love with you."

Britne's tone became emphatic. "It's not so simple, Paul."

"How do you feel for me?" Paul demanded. "Do you love me, I mean, deep down inside?"

"Of course I do, but, to be honest, right now, I'm… I'm feeling very pressured, and I don't have peace about what's happening—"

Paul sat up abruptly, cringing at the pain that shot through his body, and interrupted her. "Oh, come on, Brit," he demanded again. "I'm trying to open my heart to you. I feel like I'm gonna explode."

Britne sat up as well, almost pleading with him to understand. "So do I! But we can't let that dictate our actions."

The insecurities Paul had joked about when they first met were coming to the surface, and he was becoming argumentative and insensitive to her feelings.

"But you're turning this into something… *wrong!*"

Britne's tone was less contentious, but now she was becoming more resolute in her convictions. It was clear that he wasn't even attempting to understand her, the feelings she had inside, or the reasons why she felt as she did.

"To me… *this way*… is wrong."

Paul stood up, ignoring the pain that wracked his body. "Great! What about all this love you were just talking about?"

Britne was beside herself in disbelief. This wasn't the man she thought she had fallen in love with. He was uncaring, pretentious and insensitive. Her feelings were now a mix of horror and anger, thinking that she had so naively opened her heart to him, and allowed him into the deepest parts of her soul. How could she have been so stupid and blind not to have seen this side of him. All at once she began to doubt herself. Steve was right about him. Her heart was breaking, and she didn't know how to deal with this at all.

"That's not fair, Paul. You're taking what I believe to be a way of life, an attitude of the heart, twisting it around, and trying to manipulate me in a way that's tearing me apart."

He can't be this cold, she thought. *He's got to be able to understand how I feel.* "It's not that I don't *want* to make love to you," she continued, "because I do, very much I do. But… we've got to wait." She paused. "I *have* to wait."

"I've been waiting," Paul defended, "and very patiently, if I say so myself."

Britne was done with this line of reasoning. "I told you that you wouldn't understand. You're not trying to share your love. You're trying to take mine… selfishly, without any concern for me or how I feel."

"You're right, Brit," Paul interrupted venomously, then paused. "I don't understand."

He walked out of the room, and Britne followed him, picking up her Bible. He put his shirt on, threw the tie around his neck so it hung down both sides of his chest, and was getting himself together to leave.

"I thought we had something really special, Brit." He paused, and looked into her eyes. "Maybe I was wrong."

Britne was crushed, the breaking of her heart all but complete, and she broke down crying. "Oh, Paul, we do have something special. I just want it to stay that way."

Paul picked up his jacket, then pointed at the Ten Commandments on the mantel. "You can't force everyone to live by your rules, you know," he said bitterly.

"They're not *my* rules, Paul," she said defensively, but gently. "I didn't make them. I just try to live by them."

They stood there, looking at each other for an extended moment, each one waiting for the other to say something. It was Britne who spoke first.

"Please don't leave like this, Paul. Let's talk about it."

Paul was still bitter, but more flat. "What do you want from me? There's nothing to talk about. It's obvious, Brit…"

He thought about the *obvious* for a moment, not really sure if it was what he truly believed. All he knew was that he was angry with her, and didn't quite know why. It wasn't like she had done anything wrong. No, he was just angry, and let that anger do the talking right now.

"My love isn't good enough for you."

"I never said that, Paul, and you know it."

"You didn't have to say it, Britne. It's in the air… and it stinks."

She was almost pleading. "That's not true. I do love you."

Paul was done. "You really confuse me, you know that?"

He walked toward the door.

With that, Britne was done, too. "Believe it, or not, Paul, but I'm not doing what you ask of me *because* I love you. Don't take an act of that love, and my faith, and twist it into something negative."

Paul reached over and picked up his helmet sitting on the chair at the kitchen table, then started to open the door. He stopped, turned, and looked straight into her eyes.

"I don't know, Brit… I just don't know."

Then he was gone.

Britne stood there, at first, not understanding what had just happened. Then she dropped her Bible on the couch and ran to the door. She wanted so badly to open it, and run after him, but something inside of her wouldn't allow it. She had to be strong, and knew without a doubt that she was doing the right thing. She put her hands on the door, and laid her right cheek flat against it, as if she were listening for any audible sound, and continued to cry. Turning around, she leaned against the wall with her back, just left of the door, and slowly slid down to a sitting position, holding her knees up close to her chest. And she cried. Deep, deep down inside of her, she knew this moment would come. She thought that she was prepared for it. In none of her imagined conflicts, though, was it ever this painful. *Why, Lord… why does it have to hurt so much?*

And she cried.

Outside the door, Paul quickly moved to the left, so that she couldn't see him through the peephole. He leaned his back against the wall, and thought for a moment. Racing a million miles an hour, he couldn't begin to understand every thought that was running through his mind. None, except for one. One thought kept bouncing back and forth, slapping him upside his head. It started to drown out every other idea, word or picture that was fighting for their own survival. Just one thought. *What have I done?* The woman of his dreams, the girl that made his heart sing and dance, the one that made life seem perfect… he had just pulverized. What had he done?

He slowly slid down the wall to a sitting position, holding his knees close to his chest, ignoring any pain his body lashed out. That physical pain was nothing compared to the aching, ripping pain inside his heart. And he cried, for the second time that day. For the second time in years. What had he done? He had crushed the heart of the one he truly loved. That's what he'd done! So he sat there for a moment. And he cried.

On both sides of the wall, they each struggled with the pain and loss that neither of them were prepared for. Slowly, each one picked themselves up. Paul found his way down the hall, and out of the building; while Britne made her way back to sit on her couch. She picked up her Bible, held it tight against her heart, and then laid down and curled up. And continued to cry, from deep, deep within her soul.

COMPELLING ATTRACTION

Paul was sitting on the bank of the river, at *'The Rapids,'* listening to the *Damascus Road* CD, trying to sort through his thoughts and feelings. A couple of days had passed since his fight with Britne, and they hadn't seen each other at all. His reality was as dark as it had ever been; his best friend was dead somewhere, and his dream girl had rejected him. It seemed to him that every time he got close to someone, no matter who it might be, everything just went straight to hell. They either left, got hurt, or died. *Love,* he thought bitterly to himself. *Where's the love in all this?* He didn't see the type of love he had read about in Britne's room in any of this, or in anything. And she had rejected his love for her. *No,* he continued thinking, *there's no love in this world at all.* He did know one thing, though. He had to find Luc's body. Where, how, when... he hadn't a clue. He had to find him, though, and somehow give him a dignified memorial. *Oh happy day, love is in the air. Yeah right!*

As he sat there, listing to the music on the CD, the song that just now started grabbed his attention. He had listened to it before, and liked it, but now... today... it spoke to his heart in a whole new way. It was a soft, acoustically driven pop song... a love song... with a catchy groove and moderate tempo...

My heart skipped a beat or two
The moment that I first saw you,
The beauty in your eyes
   took my breath away.
I knew it then, I know it now
There's got to be a way, somehow,
For you to open up
   your heart to me.

Compelling attraction,
Emotional satisfaction...
I don't know what to do.
So I'll follow my heart,
And hope it doesn't break apart,
As I reach out to you.

Paul was too consumed with his thoughts to notice that someone had come up from the trail behind him, and was now standing next to him.

"I thought I'd find you here," Luc said indifferently.

Paul literally jumped up from where he was sitting, and found himself standing in the water, looking at his best friend like he was a ghost. Indeed, to Paul, he was. He stared at him until Luc started laughing uncontrollably. He didn't know how to feel... angry, happy, sad... but he turned off the CD player clipped to his belt, and got control of himself the best that he could.

"Jesus, Luc, I thought you were dead!"

"Whatever gave you that idea?" Luc asked, confused.

"Something my brother said." He stepped out of the water, grabbed Luc and hugged him. It was a long hug, a brotherly hug. And tears began to fill his eyes. "It's really great to see you!" He stepped back and looked into Luc's eyes. "You're alive!"

Still laughing, and still confused, Luc gave him the once-over. "Yeah, I am… but let me tell you, bro, *you're* not looking too good."

Paul chuckled at that, and sat back down on the bank of the river. "Fate cornered me in an alley, bro," he offered in explanation. "I should have listened to you."

Luc knew Paul too well, and could read him like a book. There was more on Paul's mind. He sat down next to his brother, in heart and soul, and offered to listen.

"You being out here, though, isn't about that alley, is it?"

"No, it isn't. You've always been able to read me, Luc."

"We've been together a long time, man."

Paul paused for a bit, then told him, "I fell hard, Luc. I let my guard down, and fell hard. Now I have this emptiness," pointing to his heart, "right here, like a vacuum that's suffocating me. I'm confused."

"Women will do that, man. All I can say is follow your heart, not your head or your pride."

"It's not so much pride, Luc, as it is identity. I don't know who I am or what I believe anymore. Nothing makes sense. My whole life is… well, backwards… I don't know, inside out."

Luc understood how his friend felt, but for different reasons. Paul didn't know it, but he'd been spending a lot of time with Steve lately. Talking. About Paul, and Tony. About life, and death. About eternity, and God. So much of what Steve had to say made a lot of sense, and he remembered the things that his parents had taught him. About love, faith, and conviction.

"Yeah, I know what you mean. It just seems like we're all caught in a series of events we really have no control over. It's not just about you and Tony, or even about innocent people dying.

It's bigger than all of this. It's bigger than all of *us*. We're just players in the game, and it's time to get out."

Paul looked over at his friend bewildered, not believing what he just heard.

"Say that again!?"

Luc continued. "Well, I've been thinking about what Steve said to Billy the other day. It sort of fit into what we've been dealing with all this time. Whatever the case, I've been feeling very uncomfortable. I just can't do this anymore, Paul. It's not really my fight anyway, and it's not yours, either.

Paul was truly stunned. Of all people to turn on him, he never would have figured Luc to be one of them.

"First Steve, and now you!"

"People change, man," Luc explained. "Steve changed, I've changed… *you've* changed." He paused. "Things aren't what they used to be, Paul. *Everyone* has changed."

Paul looked away, completely at a loss for words. Never in his life had he felt so isolated, so alone, so… *lonely*. They both just sat there looking at the river for a couple of minutes. Paul was drowning in his thoughts.

Then Luc got up. "I gotta go." With genuine love and concern in his eyes, he asked, "You okay?"

"Yeah, I'm fine," Paul answered, glancing up at his friend. "Gotta press on, eh?"

"One day at a time, bro… one day at a time. I'll see ya 'round."

"Yeah… later," Paul said, staring at the river.

Luc started to walk away, and then turned around to face Paul. "For what it's worth, Paul, I was wrong."

Paul looked over his shoulder, and up at Luc. "About what?"

"Britne. She's special, sort of like…" He thought for a moment, "a dark star."

"A what?"

"A dark star," Luc explained. "Hard to see at first, but once you find it, you never forget it." He paused, then smiled at Paul. "Well, don't be a stranger, eh?" He started to walk away.

"I won't, bro, I won't." He paused. "Luc?" Luc stopped and turned back toward Paul. "It's really great to see you."

Luc smiled again. "Later, bro!" And then he walked off.

And Paul was alone.

With his thoughts.

And he knew what he had to do. Talking to Luc always seemed to help him get a grip on what was right, what was wrong, and what the proper course of action should be—regardless of the situation. He really loved that man.

He loved Britne, too. And he had to tell her. She had to know that his heart was more than committed to her. Somehow, someway… he had to win her heart back one more time.

He hopped up with a conviction in his heart, ready to offer himself up to the woman that meant everything in the world to him. He would change his life for her. She'd *already* changed his life. He couldn't imagine another day going by without her next to him, or him next to her.

He literally ran down the path to his motorcycle and jumped onto the seat without unlocking his helmet from the side where it was attached. He felt a new freedom in his soul, and wanted to share this with the love of his heart.

He did something then that he had never done with his two-wheeled mount. With a thrust of his right leg, he kick-started this monster of a cycle, and cranked up the motor with a twist of his wrist. Sitting there before he started moving, his thoughts once again came around to the *Damascus Road* CD, and it became clear to him in a way he'd never thought of before. Each song on the recording seemed to have been written just for him, for his situation, for the questions in his heart. Every song seemed to speak to a specific circumstance in his life, and he wondered, for the first time, if Britne was right. *What are you tying to tell me?* he asked. Was God, of all people, actually attempting to speak to him, personally, intimately? Now *that* would be pretty special. *God is trying to talk to me,* he thought. *Why has it taken me so long to figure this out. God is trying to speak to me!*

He took the headphones from around his neck, slipped them back over his ears, and picked up the music where he had left off. Grabbing ahold of the handlebars and shifting his steed into first gear with the flick of his foot, he guided this beast forward into his future… a future filled with love, and devoid of the pain he had grown so accustomed to. A future that was going to be different than anything he'd known in his past.

And he cruised… listening to the music…

> *I am a man of many dreams,*
> *All of them my destiny,*
> *But all that I can do is dream of you.*
> *My life will never be the same*
> *Until you turn to me and say*
> *My love, I give my heart to you.*

> *Compelling attraction,*
> *Emotional satisfaction…*
> *I don't know what to do.*
> *So I'll follow my heart,*
> *And hope it doesn't break apart,*
> *As I reach out to you.*

THE END...

The four men stood huddled together around a roaring fire in a rusted fifty-gallon barrel, on a hilltop just beyond the view of their next big target. From this vantage, they could clearly see *Damascus Road* and the surrounding area, but were not visible to anyone below, hidden by trees and vegetation that allowed for some anonymity. The crisp, cool air forewarned of the changing season, and the night sky was clear and vibrant with an unhindered view of the star-filled heavens. Behind them were the truck and a couple of muddied dirt bikes that had seen better days.

The scene was eerie, but almost comical; the shadows of men and machine slithering amongst the branches and backdrop of the vegetation, moving in rhythm to the wind and dancing flames of the fire. It could have been a true microcosm of Hell itself, if not for the driver providing the twisted comedy of drinking a beer and roasting marshmallows.

Billy was peering through some binoculars, keeping a watchful eye on the club. The parking lot was empty, save for Steve's piece of trash little car and a van parked by the side door with equipment being unloaded. *We'll see who's in checkmate, now,* he thought. *Too bad it's not full of people.* He let the binoculars hang down by the strap around his neck, his face still swollen from the broken nose he'd received at the hospital. He warmed his hands over the barrel, careful not to let them be scorched by a molten marshmallow.

Tony and the two who had beaten Paul so badly were keeping the chill at bay with the heat from the fire, as well. Every few minutes or so, Tony would glance down at his wrist watch, obviously impatient, ready for this to be done with.

"I like Fall, y'know," the driver thought out loud. "Roasted marshmallows, cuddling weather… that sort of stuff."

"Yeah, I know what you mean, man," his friend agreed.

"The two of you get a freakin' room, already," Tony chided, "and what's with the marshmallows?"

"Hey, Tony… when's it gonna blow?" Billy inquired, raising those binoculars once again, still keeping a watchful eye on their target.

Taking another look at his watch, Tony answered, "About five minutes. Nothin's gonna be left when it's over." With a sudden outburst of anger, he vented some frustration. "We should be doing this later! Freakin' judge has lost his nerve… *nobody's* there!"

"I guess the hospital riled up too many people," the driver speculated.

"Whatever," Tony rebutted dismissively. It seemed that everything was getting all twisted and confused as of late, and he was beginning to question exactly what he was doing. "What am I doing this for any more?" he mumbled to himself.

"What did you say, Tony?" the driver asked, not really interested, but curious enough to engage him in conversation.

"Eat your freakin' marshmallows."

"Ain't it grand?" Billy yelled, drawling with delight. "I've been waitin' for this since he opened the place. There's his sister. Hooeeey! What a waste of some fine sugar. It's funny, y'know. You wait, and… Heeey! Look who's comin' to the party!" He handed Tony the binoculars and continued, excitedly, "It's your brother."

"What?" Tony asked, looking through the binoculars. Sure enough, there he was, cruising up on his bike, just pulling into the parking lot. The bike was unmistakable. And there was Britne, walking toward the front of the building. It would be a woman that brought his brother down, he thought.

The driver was excited about that, remembering the hurt Paul had put on him just a couple of days ago. "Looks like we'll kill two birds with one stone, eh, Tony?"

Tony was beside himself. "I gotta get down there." He ran to a dirt bike and cranked it up.

"Yo, Tony," the passenger warned. "You're gonna freakin' die, man."

Tony ignored the statement altogether, and addressed Billy directly. "Don't wait for me… get out of here as soon as she blows. Got it?"

Billy couldn't understand why he was doing such a thing. "What are you doing, Tony? You're nuts to go down there."

Tony was undaunted with obsession. "Just split, okay? I'll catch up with you."

Then he spun the motorcycle around and took off for the club, spewing rocks and dirt everywhere, leaving his comrades hacking in a cloud of dust.

"That dude has a death wish," the driver said, coughing and waving off some dust. Then he noticed the marshmallow he was roasting was filled with dirt. "Oh, man! He ruined it!"

Billy just stood there, shaking his head and laughing to himself.

At the club, Paul had pulled in on his signature motorcycle.

He was wearing jeans, a red T-shirt and bandana, his shades on top of his head, running shoes, his holstered gun, a sheathed knife, the CD player clipped to his belt, and the headphones.

The lot was void of all but two cars and the equipment van. Britne had just arrived, usually there early to help get the club ready for the evening's business. She was walking across the parking lot, toward the front door. Paul didn't want to freak her out completely by pulling up right next to her, so he stopped about halfway across the lot, some fifty yards from the building. He jumped from the motorcycle, not even taking the time to turn it off. He wasn't sure if he should go to her, so he stayed by his bike.

"Britne, wait!" he shouted. "Please!"

She had heard the bike's arrival, and tried to quicken her pace toward the building, not sure she even wanted to see him. Still, when he called her name, she stopped just in front of the entrance, but kept her back to him.

Paul took just a few short steps forward, but stopped again when she refused to look at him. This was going to be harder than he had thought, and he had to fight the urge to just hop back on his bike and leave outright. He knew he couldn't do that, though, and got right to the point, instead.

"I love you, Brit... I... I *need* you, Brit."

Britne wanted so badly to turn and run into his arms, to hold him and kiss him. But she also knew that she couldn't ever be the woman he apparently wanted her to be. She turned around, slowly, to face him, and addressed him with firm and resolute conviction.

"No, Paul! You don't need *me*. I can't fill the emptiness inside your heart. What you wanted the other night, you can get anywhere. Just not from me."

Paul sensed her resolve, and it invigorated him. That strong, independent determination was what really drew him to her. But more than that, it was her… her faith. Her convictions.

"I can change, Brit. I promise I can." He pleaded with her, with his eyes, for the chance to prove himself. "I will!"

Britne could see in his eyes the passion, the sincerity, and the determination. But she wasn't convinced that his heart was in the right place, and without the kind of conviction and commitment to the Lord that she knew was vital, they could very well be struggling with this dilemma again.

"But I *can't* change, and…" she paused, knowing that she couldn't give in to the desires she had for him. "I *won't*."

Steve walked up behind her, inside the glass doors. He'd also heard Paul's motorcycle arrive. Britne hadn't said much over the last couple of days, but her silence spoke louder than any words, and he knew that something had happened. He also hadn't seen the two of them together, which certainly eased his own concerns, but was odd nonetheless.

"What I believe," she continued, speaking from the depths of her heart and soul, "it's who I am, and I can not, and will not, compromise on that."

"That's cool, Brit," Paul promised. "I'll do the compromising, okay? Just please give me a chance." He started to walk toward her. "Please, let's work on this… together… you and I."

Britne was torn, her heart breaking at the sight of this man she knew to be strong and fearless begging her for a second chance. God was, after all, a God of second chances, of new beginnings. But, this wasn't about God, so far as she could see. Not for him, at least. This was about the human condition, the human heart, and desires not rooted in God's Spirit.

"I don't know, Paul, I just don't—"

Without warning, out of nowhere, a dirt bike came flying through the air from the other side of Damascus Road, to the left of where Paul was parked; through the air and over the road, the bike landed in the parking lot, and headed straight for Paul. He should have turned off his motorcycle, Paul thought, and he would have heard it coming. Then he recognized Tony as the driver, and shifted into defense mode. As Tony hauled right up to Paul, he forced the bike into a spinning, 180-degree stop. Paul had pulled his gun from the holster, and stepped in between Tony and Britne. But Tony was there for different reasons than Paul calculated.

"Don't go any closer, Paul," Tony yelled.

Paul aimed his gun directly at Tony's head, hoping to show that he truly meant business. "What do you want, Tony?"

There was something different about Tony. Something strangely different, in his eyes. There wasn't the coldness... the steely, lifeless stare. Instead, they were full of fear... and concern... and it confused Paul.

"Just get outta here," Tony yelled.

"What?" Paul asked, unable to make out what he was saying.

"Get away from here, *now!*" Tony screamed above the roar of the two motors, and said nothing more. He just hauled off.

Paul watched him for a second. Wondering. His *eyes!*

Then it hit Paul like a sledge hammer, and he realized what was about to happen.

"Britne," he shouted, turning to face her, "*Get away from there!*"

Britne was watching Tony, then looked deep into Paul's eyes when he turned around yelling at her. And she knew.

Steve came out of the building, standing just behind her at the front entrance, suspecting something was happening. Little did he know.

Paul screamed at the top of his lungs, "*Run!*"

Fear gripped her heart. She couldn't move. She couldn't breathe. She knew it the moment Paul looked at her, his eyes filled with panic. She was going to die. She started to run.

And just like that, it happened. With a deafening roar, and a tsunami of heat and flame, the building exploded, engulfing Steve completely, and tossing Britne forward like a rag doll in a tornado.

Evaporated was more descriptive. It all happened so fast, yet everything around Paul seemed to move in slow motion. The guy at the right side door flying backward, and his van flipping over on its side. Tony speeding off to the left on Damascus Road, away from the building. Every square inch of Britne's face as she tried to run toward him—her baby blue eyes, her beautiful, yet subtle, rosy-pink cheeks, the reflection of the moon on her shiny golden hair. And the panic. The panic that filled her eyes. And the pain that overtook her as the flames, heat, and glass from the front door impacted her beautiful, petite body.

Paul was thrust backward by the wave of destruction, and landed well behind his motorcycle. Pieces of the building were raining down all around him like a ticker-tape parade in New York City as he laid there, stunned and in a fog.

Slowly, he pushed himself off the ground to a sitting position, the myriad sounds of the metal, wood, concrete and glass particles continuing to fall to the ground around him. His attention first fell on the frame of what was once *Damascus Road*, flames of fire towering well above his head, smoke billowing and curling up and around the now hollow two-story shell. Then, like a knife cutting straight through his heart, he saw Britne's body fifty feet in front of him... limp, twisted, unmoving, face on the ground.

"Nooooo!" He screamed. His vision collapsed in, and the world around her disappeared completely. All he saw was her body. It seemed, for that split second, that all life came to a complete stop. Life was over as he knew it. He wanted to die.

He scrambled to his feet and ran to Britne, sliding to her body like a ballplayer grasping for home plate. The building was burning behind them. Confused, dazed, he didn't know what to do. Then he heard her moan, and his hands instinctively reached out, turning her over and pulling her into his lap. There was so much blood, and it took a couple of seconds for the pain to register in his own body. He was bleeding as well, but not from injuries sustained in the blast. The glass... so much glass... embedded into her back, cutting and slicing through the flesh on his arms and hands as he wrapped them around her body. It didn't matter right now. Nothing mattered right now, except her. As gently as his panic-stricken mind could allow, he lifted her onto his lap. Her eyes were closed. Was she alive? *I heard her moan,* he thought to himself.

Staring down at her listless body, he thought he could hear whooping and hollering in the distance. He quickly gazed at the horizon over the hills in the distance and caught a flicker of light. He heard some more... Laughing!? Celebrating!?

She made a labored, soft gasp for air, and this snapped his attention back to the one and only love of his heart. She was alive! Barely... but alive! His eyes began to well up with tears.

"Oh, God, Brit, stay with me..."

Britne cracked open her eyes, barely, and looked at him, speaking ever so softly, "Paul—"

"I'm right here, Brit." He couldn't hold back his tears as they began to fall on her face.

"I… love… you," she whispered with all of her remaining strength.

"I love you, too, babe. Oh, God, I love you, too!"

"Open… your… heart…" She winced in pain.

"Britne! Hang on… please… stay with me, Brit—"

She smiled at him. Just a whimsical, tiny, fraction of a smile. Her eyes gleamed, too. Barely visible, as if they reflected the wondrous beauty of the stars high up in the heavens, they gleamed.

"God… God… loves…"

She said no more. Her eyes were looking straight at him, right into his own eyes, deep into his soul. But the gleam was gone. Nothing was there. She was gone.

Paul stopped breathing. He moved ever closer to her face, to her eyes, and stared into them… searching, hoping, begging, praying… but finding nothing left to hold on to. Then the tears burst through as he gasped for his own air. And he cried.

Deep and silent, like a baby experiencing pain for the first time in its life. The first cry in pain, followed by that seeming eternity of breathlessness, when every new parent panics and wonders if their little child will ever utter a sound again. They wait, and wait, and wait. Then, as if gasping for their own life, the baby finally screams out in that piercing cry for help. Begging for someone to take the pain away. That's what it was like for Paul, right then and there.

And he sat there, holding her, sobbing like that little baby, broken and empty. It seemed like hours, though it was less than a minute. And with one last slither of a prayer, he leaned over and softly kissed her; then, slowly—painfully—he pulled himself away from her lips, because he had no choice. She was gone. Lifting his head away, he took one last, impossible look into her eyes, and ever so gently—tenderly—closed them with the tips of his fingers.

"I love you, Britne Nicole… girl of my dreams."

He laid her down on the ground as gently as he could, and was kneeling there beside her limp, lifeless body.

And his sobs of grief began to turn to rage.

Welling up inside of him, magma in the volcano of his soul, he turned his gaze toward Heaven and lifted his two hands as fists, and screamed.

"*Why!?*"

Then it hit him, like a bolt of lightning striking him on the spot, electricity coursing through every vein and blood vessel in his body. Anger. Hatred. Rage.

Tony, that murdering piece of white trash scum! He was getting away! He regretted, with every ounce of life he had in him, that he didn't kill Tony when he had the chance. All those opportunities, wasted on genetic loyalty. Had he done what he should've done, he reasoned with cold loathing, then Britne wouldn't be laying there, dead… empty… lifeless.

Paul knew what he was going to do, what he *had* to do. He looked at Britne's body and vowed he would avenge her. He looked over at his motor, jumped up and ran to it, the motor still running. Reaching down, he picked up his gun on the fly, and quickly holstered it. He mounted his faithful beast and cranked the accelerator handle, billowing a cloud of gray smoke from his tire as he launched forward after his prey.

Tony didn't expect Paul to come after him so soon, and it didn't take long for Paul to catch him, his bike far superior, his intent more motivating. To Tony's horror, Paul appeared, seemingly out of nowhere, right there next to him. Tony looked over at him, but Paul refused to look in his direction, instead staring straight ahead. He knew that he couldn't outrun Paul on his monster of a bike, at least not on pavement. His only real hope was to make a beeline for the terrain off road. But instead of doing what he knew would save him, he stayed there on the road, cruising next to his brother.

Waiting for the inevitable.

Wanting the inevitable.

Paul was more than willing to accommodate. Staring coldly ahead, he reached down with his right hand, removed the rifle from its holster and pointed it at Tony. He then turned to face his younger sibling, and smiled. One that betrayed the pure hatred and revenge taking root in his heart and soul. Paul wanted the last thing his brother saw on Earth to be his own smiling face, as his brain fried from the single electro-pulse put right between his eyes. With his aim dead-center true, he began to pull back on the trigger.

Suddenly, without warning, Paul was blinded by the brightest, whitest, and most brilliant of lights. He heard the sounds of a crash.

Then… nothing.

THE DREAM

The illusion, a pool of water floating above the desert floor, formed a translucent, wavy barrier between what was clearly seen, and that which was not; a contrast of refreshing coolness in the midst of extreme heat.

Paul ignored the illusion, though, as he ran forward in urgent desperation, more aware, instead, of the pounding of his heart within his chest. Constricting with every breath, the muscles in his throat began to rob him of much needed oxygen, and the heat emanating from the arid soil caused his lungs to burn like fire. If that wasn't bad enough, the soles of his feet were blistering inside his high-tech running shoes, as each jarring step swallowed yet another cubic inch of sand. The jeans he was wearing impeded every stride he took, slowing his progress forward to what seemed a snail's pace. His red T-shirt was soaked in sweat, as was the bandana covering his head. He continued to push his pace, reaching deep within to find that intestinal fortitude his father so often spoke of as he was growing up. Adorned in black riding gloves, his hands and arms pumped like pistons. The hunting knife in its sheath rattled and slapped his thigh, while the gun holstered to his left side pierced the muscle tissue between his ribs.

Suddenly, his body coiled in pain as a cramp formed in his gut, and he came to an abrupt stop, wheezing and gasping for air.

Though in better shape than most men his age, his body was now betraying him.

The mirrored, black-framed sunglasses covered his eyes as they darted back and forth, scanning the blazing surroundings with fatal urgency. The shades also exaggerated the sweat flowing from his forehead. Blood was trickling from his nose and the corner of his mouth. His thoughts were racing out of control, rational and irrational, swirling together in a vortex of panic and fear; yet, he was keenly focused on the single, primary task of getting away. Quickly glancing behind, his gaze locked onto the mass of small figures, warped and distorted by the waves of rising heat, moving in his direction.

Any irrational thoughts he may have entertained were immediately dismissed as the internal drive for self-preservation... to survive... regained control, and he took off once again. No matter how fast he ran, the mass of figures grew larger as they began to close the gap. Outfitted much differently than Paul, they were better suited to their more primitive surroundings, and apparently more prepared for this method of pursuit. Swords brandished and shields ready, they ran in unison... and tired slowly. Paul looked back again to see them closing in on him, and realized just how much out of his element he really was. How is it possible, he thought, that Roman Soldiers would be chasing him? Without warning, he tripped and stumbled to the desert surface. Rolling over, he glanced back again to see the Romans bearing down on him. Scrambling to his feet, he lunged forward in a sprint for his life. He could hear the sound of the soldier's armor behind him, and reached even deeper to find the strength to keep going, and then fell again... a bad fall...

✳✳✳

THOUGHTS

Truth is sometimes difficult to accept, and, sometimes, it takes a broken heart before we're ready to hear it. When we do listen, though, that truth can set us free, and our lives will change forever...

GETHSEMANE

It was the same dream… the same one he always had. The running, the Roman Soldiers, the heat, the fear.

Paul awoke, like always, startled and disoriented, gasping for air, and panicked. This time, though, something just wasn't right. Everything felt different. He wasn't in his room, nor was he anywhere that could remotely be recognized.

Then it dawned on him abruptly, like biting the inside of his cheek. He checked himself over, finding all his parts intact. Frantically he looked around, searching for his motorcycle. It was nowhere to be seen. *Where is it? Where's Tony? The road?* Now he was beginning to freak out. *Where am I?* This wasn't home, that's for sure.

He scanned the surrounding area again, wondering if he'd died and ventured into Purgatory, or Shangri La, or Neverland.

Get it together Paul, he thought to himself. Now wasn't the time to lose himself in fantastical insanity. One more time he looked at his environment, trying to ascertain exactly where he was. In a park of some sort. Or an orchard. Or a garden. It was peacefully cool, and smelled different, too. Fresh, clean, sort of musky, but untainted by the mechanisms of refined propulsion.

How did he get here, though… wherever *here* actually was? Slowly, he stood to his feet, still trying to get his bearings right, and began to walk around rather aimlessly. The vegetation was unlike anything he'd seen before, the trees sprouting branches in all sorts of directions; curling, twisting, rolling, with thin leaves, and black berries of some sort. Meandering amongst the trees, he took a closer look. They weren't berries. They were… olives! He was in an orchard filled with Olive trees. *That's odd,* he thought. Of course, everything right now was odd, and he needed to figure out where he was and how to get home.

Then he heard a voice, and ducked for cover. He closed his eyes, and held his breath, trying to get a fix on the location of the voice.

Silence.

Come on, come on!

More silence.

Then he heard it again, a soft voice, off to his right. Staying low to the ground, he crawled through the trees in that direction. He came upon a group of huge rocks, a little more in the open than he was comfortable with, so he stayed low and in the shadows of the trees.

Inching around the perimeter of the cluster, he spotted a man leaning with his back against one of the larger stones, clothed in a most unusual outfit. He was normal enough physically—rugged looking; fit; light, medium-length hair; not much of a beard, maybe a week's growth—but he was wearing a robe of some sort, taupe in color, and tied at the waist with a rope.

The man was in obvious distress and was sweating profusely. He was speaking to someone else. Paul moved around as stealthily as possible, trying to get a better view of the man and his companion. He settled behind a tree that had branches laying low to the ground, offering him some cover. Upon closer observation, Paul could see he was sweating heavily, something red.

No way, Paul thought. He squinted his eyes, peering intently through the shadows, into the soft, nearly imperceptible light that surrounded this man. *Yes, that's exactly what it is. Blood!*

How bizarre… how incredibly bizarre!

It *was* blood he was sweating. Paul's mind was racing, his thoughts rambling out of control. *It can't be,* he thought. *It isn't possible. Absolutely no way!* He decided to lay low, and listen as intently as he could to what this man was saying. He looked around, and didn't see anyone else near him. *Who's he talking to?* When he heard the man's words, he wondered—no, he *knew*—who this man was. Yet, it couldn't be.

"I've done all you've ever asked of me, Father," Jesus said. "I left my family, lived a life with no home… slept on this ground. And the friends you've given me, they followed me every step of the way. How can I leave them?"

He paused, and Paul could hear him crying, as well.

"I'm afraid, Father, I'm afraid! I don't want to die."

He paused again.

"If only I could pass this cup you've poured for me… I love you, with all my heart and soul… I do."

Again, he paused. He appeared to be in deep contemplation, and had stopped crying. Wiping his face with both sleeves of his tunic, which left faint red stains on the material, he continued with apparent resolve.

"Your will, Father… *your* will… not mine… be done."

Paul didn't realize that he was leaning forward on his hands and elbows, listening ever intently, and he snapped a small twig. He laid as flat and low as he could, still watching the man in the light, who looked over in his direction. No. He looked *precisely* where Paul was resting.

"I *will* obey you, Father," he continued, making direct eye contact with Paul as he spoke.

Paul was completely out of sorts now, his breathing quickening, and he laid his face flat to the ground, hoping desperately to find refuge behind the tree branches.

"Please, come out," Jesus requested. "I sure could use the company."

Paul clung to the ground he occupied, unable to move a single muscle. He gritted his teeth and waited for all hell to break loose. But, as he waited there, it didn't. And actually, his body relaxed in a way he couldn't understand, and peace seemed to fill his mind. That voice, it was so gentle, filled with a tenderness that defied the very circumstances surrounding them both. He looked up in the direction of the man, who was looking back at Paul with a subtle, yet comforting, smile.

So, without fear keeping him down, he climbed up from the ground, first to his hands and knees, then to his feet. And he stepped out from the shadows of the trees toward the man. Tentatively, he moved forward, taking small steps… cautiously looking around, but still not afraid.

Moving ever closer, he stopped just on the fringes of the tree line. Looking up, Paul could see the stars glittering beautifully in the night sky, but no moon. Yet, looking back at the man, he could still make out that barely visible aura of radiance. And he waited, just looking at the man with curiosity and anticipation.

"Hi, Paul," Jesus said rather casually, still sitting against the rock, "are you okay?"

Paul looked at him quizzically. "Yes, thank you." Then, realizing he was greeted by name, he asked sheepishly, "How… how'd you know my name?"

"I've known you your whole life, my brother."

"Yeah, right, give me a break."

"No, really," Jesus replied. "I was there... I was there when you were born... just like I'm here with you now."

"Ha!" Paul exclaimed, coming to the realization—he thought—that none of this was actually happening. "But you're not really here, 'cause this is just another dream."

"Are you sure of that?"

"Don't play mind games with me," Paul warned. "I'm not in the mood."

Jesus was unaffected by Paul's attempt at bravado, and replied evenly with that same subtle, yet comforting, smile. "I don't play with people's minds, Paul... I... *enlighten* them."

"Are you one of those Krishna people?" Paul asked with a tinge of sarcasm.

"Actually," Jesus said, "in their own misguided way... they're seeking *me*."

"I've heard of people like you," Paul snarled.

"Paul, stop it. You know who I am."

"I've never met you before in my life."

"Not like this, no, but we've met, on many occasions... and you *do* know who I am. You figured it out over there," Jesus said, pointing back to the trees where he had been hiding. "Besides, you actually speak my name quite often. Well, you *use* it... like a filthy word."

"I'm outta here," Paul blurted, putting his hands up, looking left and right for some sort of exit route.

"And where will you go?"

"I don't know, but away from you."

"Go ahead," Jesus said, shaking his head in subtle disappointment. Slowly, he climbed to his feet. Once again, he wiped his brow with the sleeves of his tunic, and more red stains appeared. He took a few steps in Paul's direction, then stopped. "Run away. That's all you've done your whole life, never stopping—just for a moment—to listen to what I was saying to you."

"What do you want from me?" Paul asked, arms spread in exasperation.

"Nothing… and everything. Your love, your heart, your life."

"Man," Paul whispered to himself, as he turned to walk away, "this is the most bizarre dream, yet."

"But it's not a dream," Jesus rebutted, "and in your heart, you know that. You just don't want to…" Jesus paused, for effect, "face the music."

Paul stopped, not really sure what to do or where to go, but refused to turn around.

Jesus continued. "You can't keep running away. It's just you and me now, and there's nowhere you can run any more. You have to decide, once and for all." He paused again. "And you *will* make a choice, one way or the other. Even if you don't choose, well… you've still chosen." He stopped for a moment, and allowed the silence to speak for him.

"So, Paul, what's it going to be?"

Paul still refused to look at Jesus, contemplating what was just said to him. It made sense, and he understood what Jesus meant. He'd known that for much longer than he was willing to admit, right now, but knew it nonetheless.

While Paul was being stubborn, Jesus turned and walked away. He had more pressing issues to attend to at the moment.

Paul still wasn't convinced he wasn't having another stupid dream. Feeling emboldened by that thought, he turned around defiantly. "Why must I choose between you and… hey… hey… where'd you go? Hey!"

Paul took off running after him, having absolutely no clue where he was going. He circled the cluster of rocks a couple of times, feeling very frustrated and disoriented. Then he stopped and listened, closing his eyes, figuring he might be able to hear a sound that would clue him in as to where to go. And he did! On the other side of the rocks. So, he took off in that direction, running as fast as he could through this unfamiliar territory. After a while, he spotted Jesus walking toward a group of men huddled together, laying on the ground. They were dressed similarly to Jesus, but with a bit more color to their clothing. He followed him, hiding nearby behind a thick, burly tree, as Jesus started speaking to the men.

"Are you still asleep?" Jesus asked rhetorically. "Wake up, all of you. Come on, wake up." He wasn't angry, but instead spoke in the tone parents use when waking their children early in the morning. "The time of my betrayal into the hands of sinners is upon us. Let's go. Get up."

The men climbed to their feet, groggy and still half asleep, when another group, numbering about a dozen, approached from off to Paul's right, carrying torches, clubs and spears. Again, their dress was similar to the others, but some were wearing leather chest armor and leather helmets, while a few were dressed much more ornately. *Guards and priests,* Paul figured.

About ten or fifteen feet behind them was a smaller group of about six men, and Paul definitely recognized them. They wore the uniforms of Roman soldiers, exactly like the ones in his dream, and were brandishing swords. They seemed rather disinterested, and gave very little attention to the matter at hand. They actually appeared to be making fun of the lot of them.

Paul felt his heart rate increase as he stood there watching this unfold, and his mind began to race ahead. If this were his dream, then why so much more detail than the other times. *Wait,* he thought. He already *had* that dream, just before he woke up here. He was really confused now. *What is going on,* he thought.

As the priests and guards arrived, one of Jesus' friends approached him. "What's happening, Master?" Paul heard him ask.

"My betrayer has arrived," Jesus answered, turning his head to look directly at Paul in the same uncanny way he had earlier, knowing exactly where he was hiding. But this time, his look wasn't so tender. He gazed into Paul's eyes with pain and sorrow filling his own.

Paul immediately felt guilt and anger well up inside himself. *Why did he look at me like that? I'm not betraying him! Is that what you're saying? That's preposterous! I didn't betray you,* he yelled to himself. *I didn't betray you!*

Just then, a man wearing no armor stepped forward from amongst the guards and priests, and timidly stopped after a couple of feet.

"Move!" said the group leader, giving him a shove.

The man walked up to Jesus, and attempted to kiss him, only to have Jesus stop him.

"Do you betray me with a *kiss,* Judas?"

"Rabbi!" Judas painfully responded.

"Then," Jesus said, "do what you've come to do, my friend."

Judas kissed him on both cheeks, and then stepped away, looking down at the ground in shame. Jesus lifted Judas' chin, and looked at him with a smile on his face; a hurting, knowing… loving smile. Judas looked up at him with tears in his eyes, and turned away, unable to bear the burden of what he had just done.

Paul was transfixed by what he was watching. His heart was aching, too. Was he really witnessing what he thought he was?

Jesus then turned his attention to the guards, and his demeanor changed dramatically. Gone was the tenderness and the smile, replaced with a stern and focused determination. It was clear that he knew why they were there.

"Who is it you want?"

"Jesus of Nazareth!" The group leader replied.

"That is I," he said candidly.

To Paul's amazement, the entire group stepped back at his response, throwing their arms up in unison as if covering their eyes and faces, and cowered at his very words. Many of them stumbled and fell over each other, yelling out in fear. Then it dawned on him. Jesus was in total control of the situation, and these men were powerless to do anything about it.

Jesus stood there waiting for them to act, to do something, growing ever more impatient and irritated. "I asked… who is it you want!?"

"The man Jesus!" said the group leader.

"I've told you, *I AM* Jesus."

"Get him!" barked the leader to his men, but even then Jesus maintained complete control.

"If it's me you want, then let these men go. They've done nothing wrong."

"Let's go," commanded the leader, trying not to lose face with his Roman chaperones. "Take him!"

Two of the guards approached Jesus and reached for him, when out of the group of Jesus' friends jumped a man with a sword.

Paul was breathless, absorbed totally in the human drama

playing out before his eyes. He quickly thought back to himself trapped in the alley with Tony, just a couple of nights ago.

Before he could be absorbed in those memories, the man with the sword lunged at the guard on Jesus' left, swinging his sword in a downward arch. He struck the guard on the side of the head, and Paul watched his left ear pop off his head. The guard fell to the ground, screaming and holding his head.

At the sight of a fight, the Romans' attention perked up, and they started to enter the fray. Without hesitating, Jesus stepped right into their path, and held up only his hand.

"No!" he said, and they stopped immediately.

He then turned to his friend. "Put down the sword, Peter. Have you learned nothing? He who lives by the sword will die by the sword! Do not resist any longer."

Then Paul saw Jesus do the most amazing thing. He picked up the ear that was lying on the ground, and gently placed it on the left side of the guard's head, who was laying on the ground, crying in agony. After just a few seconds, the man's sobbing ceased, and Jesus leaned over and whispered something in his ear.

While still caring for the guard, Jesus continued to speak to Peter with compassion and patience. "I could call upon my Father to send thousands of angels, if I desired…"

Pausing, he smiled at the guard, whose ear was now reattached and completely healed. "You will be fine, Malchus."

He lifted Malchus to his feet, and the two of them hugged passionately. The cries of agony only moments ago were replaced with shouts of joy and laughter. Every single man there—from Jesus' friends, to the guards and priests, to the Roman soldiers—stood there speechless and astonished. Malchus looked at them all, then ran quickly out of the orchard, leaving his spear there on the ground, wanting to keep the attention away from himself and avoid being questioned.

Paul watched all this with the same astonishment, and could only stand there in awe of what was happening. He saw it with his own eyes, yet still couldn't believe what he just witnessed. Out here, in this place so alien to him, everything in his own life seemed so... so irrelevant. He'd never experienced anything like what he was seeing. Then he thought of Britne. His feelings were so mixed up. He missed her, and loved her. But she... she seemed like a distant memory right now. How could that be? And why didn't she say something more than she did?

Again, Jesus took control of the moment, continuing with Peter, but actually speaking to everyone there.

"But, then, how would the scriptures be fulfilled?" With a wave of his hand, he indicated his impatience, and continued, "Enough of this."

He turned to the guards and priests, rebuking them for their hypocrisy. "Am I leading a rebellion that you come after me with clubs and swords? What a bunch of hypocrites... I taught in the temple courts everyday, but you wouldn't lay a hand on me, then. This is your moment, though, when darkness reigns, and the scriptures are fulfilled."

The leader had had enough. "Take him *now!*"

The temple guards surrounded Jesus, and bound his hands, and began to get violent with him. All of his friends ran off as he was led away.

This left Paul completely at a loss for words. *Cowards*, he thought. *All of you.* Who were these men, that they would abandon their friend? *Man, Luc would never have turned on me like that.*

A Roman soldier came up as they began to lead Jesus away,

holding a young boy about sixteen or so, and somewhat frail, wearing nothing but a cloth over his loins.

"Look what I got here," said the soldier.

The boy broke free, losing his cloth in the process, and ran away naked. The Romans broke out laughing.

"Let him go," barked the leader, "he is shamed as it is."

All the laughter and the flames from the torches were a catalyst that transported Paul's thoughts back to the parking lot at *Damascus Road*. He remembered the dying words of Britne, laying there in his arms, and the laughter off in the distance. Tears began to well up as the emotions started to build inside of him. He was shaken from his reverie as the boy sprinted past him, startling him, rousing him to movement.

That wasn't good, because the leader of the Romans spotted him.

"Wait. Who's that?"

"Who?" one of the soldiers asked, still laughing, "Where?"

"Over there, in the trees. He sure looks different."

Paul panicked, and took off running back in the direction that he had come from.

The leader selected three soldiers. "You three, after him. And when you catch him, bring him directly to me."

The three took off in hot pursuit of Paul, who wasted little time in his retreat. He didn't run; he sprinted. Twisting, curling, jumping, stumbling... he kept going, knowing his life was as good as over if they caught him. But he didn't know where he was going, or *where* he could *go*. These trees weren't helping, either, reaching out for him like hands from the dark. *Don't look back,* he screamed in thought, *don't look back. Keep going. Just keep going. Run... run... RUN!*

And so he did.

BACK ON THE FARM

Britne was kissing him, tenderly, when she backed away to look into his eyes. He reached out to her, slowly, caressing her cheek, and she closed her eyes. Leaning in again, she touched her lips to his. How beautiful she was. Her smell... so... so... musky? She proceeded to lick his face as her image faded away, and light crept in...

Paul gradually opened his eyes, just as a shadow enveloped his head, and a huge, wet, musky tongue lathered his face with saliva. Two large brown nostrils blocked his vision. He opened his eyes, wide with alarm, as the tongue began another descent. He jumped to his elbows and backpedaled as fast as he could, to see a cow standing over him. His sudden movement startled the animal, which grunted and did its own version of the two-step in the opposite direction.

"*Uch,*" he said, wiping his face. "Sorry, Elsie, but that's *not* my idea of a good morning kiss."

He then realized he was in a stable, where he managed to hide as he evaded the soldiers the night before. He scrambled to his feet, wiped himself off, and took a quick look around. Walking over to the doorway, he peered outside and saw even more farm animals, and a cart. The clouds in the sky reflected a soft orange, indicating the earliest minutes of dawn, and the air was refreshing to his tired and weary body.

From behind him, a woman's voice, sharp and angry, pierced the charm of the morning.

"Hey!" said the woman.

Shocked and surprised, he spun around to see an older woman holding a very mean looking pitchfork, with a young boy at her side, adorned in Middle Eastern peasant clothing. "What are you doing here?" she demanded.

"Calm down, lady," said Paul. "I don't even know where *here* is."

"This is my farm," she asserted, "and you don't belong here. Who are you?"

"My name's Paul, and I'm not gonna hurt you."

The woman jabbed the pitchfork at him with the ferocity of someone who'd had to do this before. "I'm sure you won't. What do you want?"

"Chill out, lady," Paul said. "I don't want anything, believe me. Look, I'm very lost. Can you tell me where I am?"

She kept her pitchfork at the ready, but backed off a bit. "About an hour's walk from the city."

"City?" Paul was elated. "Great, what city?"

"Jerusalem. Where else?" She looked at him like he was a complete idiot.

"Jerusalem? In Israel?" He asked, confused.

"Judea." She looked him over. "My, you're a strange one. Funny clothes, funny accent. Where are you from?"

"The United States."

The boy looked at him funny. "What for?"

"What?"

"What?" the woman asked.

Paul tilted his head, perplexed. "What?"

"What!?" She screamed in exasperation.

"United?" the boy asked curiously.

"Who?" Paul asked, confused at all this.

"You!"

"Me?"

"Yes."

Paul rolled his eyes, and looked at the woman, feeling like he was in the middle of a bad vaudeville act. "Lady, what's he talking about?"

"Who knows anymore?" she said, shaking her head.

"Look," Paul said. "I'm just gonna go my own way… which way to Jerusalem?"

"West."

"West?" Paul had no sense of direction here.

"That way," she indicated with a jab of her pitchfork.

Paul wanted to be sure. "That way?"

"That's what I said." She'd had about enough of him. "Now get out of here," she said, jabbing the pitchfork at him, "before I send you to the grave."

"Chill, lady… no worries." He looked at her, raising his hands in submission. "West, about an hour?"

She jabbed at him again. "Yes, now *get!*"

Paul left in the direction she pointed, and she walked to the doorway behind him, watching as he ventured toward the city.

"Young people, today," she said to herself. "What's the world coming to?"

She turned around and walked back inside the stable, slapping the boy on the back of his head as she passed him.

JERUSALEM

The farm lady was right, Paul thought. It took him about an hour to get to the city. He was wearing his sunglasses, as it was now mid-morning, and the sun was very bright. Hundreds of people filled the streets, accompanied by a myriad of animals. It seemed to be very festive, and people were bartering and trading at the many small booths and mats that lined the edges of the avenues. A good many of the men were carrying lambs or sheep on their shoulders, often accompanied by women or young boys carrying birds, flat breads or some other sort of item.

Everyone seemed to be looking at him in the strangest of ways, which made sense to Paul. After all, he didn't look anything like them, and was dressed differently than any of them had probably ever seen; he figured he wasn't exactly fitting in with the crowd.

As if on cue, he was spotted by some Roman Soldiers, the same three he had eluded the night before, coincidentally.

"There he is!" one of them yelled.

They weren't very effective in covert tactics, Paul noted, and took off when he saw them. He pushed frantically through the crowd, then turned a corner onto an empty path, and looked over his shoulder to keep an eye out for the soldiers. Turning his attention to the path ahead of him, he bolted for freedom… right into a dead end.

He stopped, arms out to his sides in frustration. "What's with the dead ends?"

He turned to face his pursuers.

The three soldiers ran past the alley, but quickly came back to it.

"I told you I saw him here," said one of the soldiers. They drew their swords, spread out just enough to keep Paul hemmed in, and began walking toward him.

Paul was feeling pretty desperate at this point, and couldn't help but remember his rendezvous with this same fate the other night. Frantically looking for a way out, he realized he had his gun. He quickly pulled it from its holster, and leveled it in front of him at the soldiers.

"Stop, right there."

The soldiers just laughed at him. "Is that a rock?" said one of them, holding his sword in attack position. "That won't help you here."

"Dudes… *stop!*" Paul warned them emphatically.

The soldiers continued to advance, laughing even harder at the absurdity of this man. When they were fifteen feet away, he fired his electro-pulse gun three times; once in front, and once, each, to the left and right, hitting the building on either side.

It was a weapon far beyond their ability to comprehend. *Harnessed lightning?* They were completely unprepared, aghast at what flew across the air in their direction. Ducking, jumping, twisting, and screaming, they literally ran over each other, finally ending up flat on the ground.

Paul took full advantage of this opportunity, hurdling himself over their bodies and running off as fast as he could.

The soldiers were beside themselves, and began to climb to their feet when they were sure he was gone.

"What in the name of the gods was that?" One of them asked in astonishment.

"Only the *gods* know!" a second one explained.

"And obviously, the gods are with him," chimed the third. "I didn't see him… did you?"

"Not me!" said the first soldier.

"See who?" agreed the second.

Paul didn't have any idea where he was, where to go, or how to get there. Checking behind him sporadically to ensure he was, for the time being, free of the soldiers, he scurried into what looked like a safe little cubby hole in the wall of a rather large building. Sitting there, crammed in as tight as he could be, his body began to complain that he was wearing it down. Gradually his eyelids became heavy, and he started to fall asleep. How he longed to be back home, with Luc and Missy… and Brit—

He shot straight up, hitting his head on the top of this little hole, at the cry of a man in terrible pain. There came a second yell, and then a third.

Paul crawled out of his cubby to investigate. Staying close to the wall, he scurried along to his right until he heard what sounded like multiple cracking whips, followed by a grunt. He followed the sound, which was obviously a painful beating, as it got louder and louder. The suffering he heard became quite unsettling the closer he got to it. Inching along, he finally approached the end of the wall and peered around the corner, into an open forum of sorts, where a man was tied, dangling from a bar straddling two poles in the center. A Roman soldier was on either side of the man, sadistically enjoying this barbaric torture. It was a horrible sight to see, and he quickly retreated back around the corner. Another lash, and another grunt.

Cautiously, he peeked around the edge of the wall again to see the weapon slash this man again. *What are they using?* It had a wood handle, and contained numerous strands of what looked like leather, about twelve to eighteen inches in length. He squinted to get a closer look, and each strand appeared to be integrated with fragments of metal and bone. Another lash across the back. *They're ripping him apart! My god,* he thought, *this place is worse than home. Do they never stop?* The man turned his head and looked in his direction.

Paul recognized him. *That's Jesus!* He pulled his gun, instinctively, and was about to shoot the two soldiers that were whipping him, when Jesus looked straight into his eyes. Ever so faintly, he shook his head "*no*," just before he was lashed across the back, and he squinted in much pain. Then, another lash came across Jesus' back. The strips of leather, metal and bone ripped into his flesh, tearing off chunks of skin and muscle… and again… and again. He looked away. It was horrible.

Paul was in complete turmoil, as lash upon lash was dealt on Jesus. He wanted so badly to stop this torture, and *could have* with but a few short bursts of his gun. But Jesus wouldn't allow it. *Why!? Why is he doing this? Why is he taking this inhuman punishment? Why?*

Finally, the soldiers grew weary and stopped, their breathing hard and fast. Paul peeked around the corner again to see what was happening. The soldiers were exhausted, and sat down to rest their arms. Their commander ordered the end of the beating.

"Cut him down," he barked.

Jesus was cut down from the framework he'd been tied to and he fell to the ground.

Another soldier came up to him, carrying a crown, with thorns at least two inches in length. "Let's put this on," he said, laughing robustly. "Every king deserves a crown." Pulling Jesus up to a sitting position, the soldier positioned the crown of thorns on his head. He was careless in his revelry, though, and one of the thorns penetrated completely through his hand.

He screamed in pain.

The commander saw this, and was livid. "You stupid idiot!" he screamed. "We could all be executed for an injury like that to yourself. Go quickly, clean the wound… and pray to the gods that we're not called upon for any serious duty."

The injured soldier quickly departed, and the commander turned to see the other soldiers bowing in mockery before Jesus.

"Hail, King of the Jews."

This infuriated the commander.

"Quit screwing around," he barked. "I won't be flogged for you scum."

He kicked one of the soldiers hard across the face just to set an example.

"Take him to the hill," he commanded.

Paul looked away in utter despair. His heart was breaking, and there was nothing he could do. He sat there motionless… numb… horrified. Nothing he had ever seen could compare to the beating he just witnessed. Not the hospital. Not the club. Nothing! He holstered his gun, and took one more look around the corner. The soldiers were dragging Jesus away, like a filthy carcass, by his feet. Paul turned away and left the scene, a tear rolling down his cheek beneath his glasses.

CALVARY

In the meantime, the three Roman soldiers looking for Paul had now become five, and they were working their way through the marketplace, making no effort whatsoever to be polite. One of them spotted Paul sneaking around some of the booths.

"I see him!" the soldier said.

"Where?" another asked.

"Over there, by the money-changers"

Paul was beside himself. Exhausted and numb, he was wandering aimlessly, struggling to get a grip on his feelings and emotions. Looking around at all the people, he wondered if any of them were aware of—or even cared about—what had just taken place. Out of the corner of his eye, he caught the reflection of the sun off of something to his left. Glancing over, he spotted the group of soldiers pointing at him. He was worn out, and didn't know how much more of this he could take. They started in his direction, and he took off running.

"Curse the gods! He saw us!"

"Get him!"

They took off after him.

Paul had a pretty good head start on them, and was blazing a path through the city streets. Looking behind him as he rounded a corner, he smashed into one of the booths, knocking it down.

He fell to the ground... a hard fall, knocking the air out of his lungs. But he got up quickly and continued running away.

The merchant of the booth lifted himself from the pile that was once his business, cursing at Paul as he ran off into the distance, waving his fist high in the air.

"Come back here, you Roman pig!"

Just as he turned around to clean up of his humble workplace, the Roman soldiers came sprinting around the turn and plowed him over, causing a massive pile-up as they fell on top of each other.

Paul continued to run. He was growing more weary and exhausted. The heat and running were taking their toll. An illusion, a pool of water floating above the desert floor, formed a translucent, wavy barrier between what was clearly seen and that which was not; a contrast of refreshing coolness in the midst of extreme heat.

Paul ignored the illusion, though, as he ran forward in urgent desperation, more aware, instead, of the pounding of his heart within his chest. Constricting with every breath, the muscles in his throat began to rob him of much needed oxygen, and the heat emanating from the arid soil caused his lungs to burn like fire. If that wasn't bad enough, the soles of his feet were blistering inside his high-tech running shoes, as each jarring step swallowed yet another cubic inch of sand. The jeans he was wearing impeded every stride he took, slowing his progress forward to what seemed a snail's pace. His red T-shirt was soaked in sweat, as was the bandana covering his head. He continued to push his pace, reaching deep within to find that intestinal fortitude his father so often spoke of as he was growing up. Adorned in black riding gloves, his hands and arms pumped like pistons.

The hunting knife in its sheath rattled and slapped his thigh, while the gun holstered to his left side pierced the muscle tissue between his ribs.

Suddenly, his body coiled in pain as a cramp formed in his gut, and he came to an abrupt stop, wheezing and gasping for air. Though in better shape than most men his age, his body was now betraying him.

The mirrored, black-framed sunglasses covered his eyes as they darted back and forth, scanning the blazing surroundings with fatal urgency. The shades also exaggerated the sweat flowing from his forehead. Blood was trickling from his nose and the corner of his mouth. His thoughts were racing out of control, rational and irrational, swirling together in a vortex of panic and fear; yet, he was keenly focused on the single, primary task of getting away. Quickly glancing behind, his gaze locked onto the mass of small figures, warped and distorted by the waves of rising heat, moving in his direction.

Any irrational thoughts he may have entertained were immediately dismissed, as the internal drive for self-preservation… to survive… regained control, and he took off once again. No matter how fast he ran, the mass of figures grew larger as they began to close the gap. Outfitted much differently than Paul, they were much better suited to their more primitive surroundings, and apparently more prepared for this method of pursuit. Swords brandished and shields ready, they ran in unison… and tired slowly. Paul looked back again to see them closing in on him, and realized just how much out of his element he really was. *How is it possible,* he thought, *that Roman soldiers are chasing me?* Without warning, he tripped and stumbled to the desert surface. Rolling over, he glanced back again to see the Romans bearing down on him. Scrambling to his feet, he lunged forward in a sprint for his life. He could hear the sound of the soldier's armor behind him, and reached even deeper to find the strength to keep going, and then fell again… a bad fall… but he got up and continued, ignoring the pain of his body, driven by the pain of his heart.

He rounded another bend in the street, and literally came up against a traffic jam. Not the kind he was familiar with, but one just the same. A horde of people filled the street, moving along a path that ran perpendicular to the one he was on. Taking a quick glance behind him, he didn't see the soldiers, and squeezed into the crowd.

Finally, he had a way of truly escaping the soldiers. Slowly, the crowd inched its way forward. There were so many of them… more than Paul imagined could fit into such a small alleyway. He couldn't tell where he was, but the elevation seemed to be changing, and he thought he was going uphill. Eventually, the crowd began to spread out into a wider area. Continuing to keep a vigilant watch behind him for the soldiers, he noticed three poles about twelve feet high, at the crest of a hill to his right.

The middle pole was empty, but the two on the outside had men on them, tied to a cross bar. He heard a pounding sound, like that of a hammer, followed by a loud roar from part of the crowd. It was coming from over by the poles. Then, there was more hammering, and another roar. He squinted through the afternoon sun, grateful for the shades he was wearing. He saw a third man lifted up and his cross bar put on the middle pole, and watched in horror as some soldiers hammered a spike through his ankles. The man screamed in pain as the huge nail went through his ankles, but was drowned out by another roar of approval from the crowd.

Bloody, beaten and naked, his body was shredded, his face swollen and discolored. From where Paul was, he could hear wheezing and gurgling, and every attempt made to breathe was terribly labored, and shallow. And he was naked! People all around him were laughing, and pointing, and mocking. One of the other men on a cross spit in his direction. It was then that he noticed who it was on the middle cross.

That's Jesus, he exclaimed to himself. *My God, he's barely recognizable.*

Paul quickly sat down, grabbed a sheet from one of the people in the crowd to cover himself up, and blended in with them. By now the soldiers had made their way into the crowd, and he watched them fearfully as they meandered about searching for him. Soon they, too, became engrossed in what was going on, and stopped the search momentarily, caught up in the executions taking place before their eyes.

It seemed like hours had passed, and Paul had become much like the rest of the crowd, onlookers in this macabre expression of human brutality. He was troubled by what he was watching. Not just the torture and sadistic killing of Jesus, but also the coldness and detachment of the people. With the exception of a small group of people up near the crosses, they seemed to be enjoying all of this.

The soldiers had joined in some kind of mockery of Jesus, and they appeared to be splitting up the garments that Jesus had been wearing.

Paul became aware of the CD still clipped to his belt. Unable to move around for fear of being noticed, he covertly took the time to listen to it... there underneath the cover of his sheet...

> *I know a man,*
> *a very special man,*
> *Who lived long ago.*
> *Now, this man*
> *Traveled throughout the land*
> *Sharing his message of love.*
>> *But those of authority*
>> *they feared his following.*
>> *He could steal the power*
>> *of their hierarchy.*
>> *So they devised a way*
>> *To put this man away,*
>> *and end a danger to their dynasty.*
>
>> *Calvary*
>> *an end and a new beginning*
>> *Calvary*
>> *the dawn of a brand new age.*
>
> *Twelve paths to choose.*
> *One man sang the blues*
> *The hang-man has stolen his soul.*
> *Ten ways to lose.*
> *One man changed the rules.*
> *Love is greater than gold.*
>> *But most of society*
>> *They fear the chance to be*
>> *Part of His chosen family.*
>> *Walk in darkness or in light.*
>> *Choose the way, that's your right.*
>> *The day will be here*
>> *when we all will see.*

*Calvary
an end and a new beginning
Calvary
the dawn of a brand new age.*

Paul heard Jesus' feeble voice coming from the cross. "I'm thirsty... I'm thirsty." He saw some soldiers whooping it up near the crosses, and strained to hear what they were saying.

"Give him some of this vinegar," said one of the soldiers, laughing and very proud of himself for thinking of the idea.

"No... let's see if Elijah will help him," said a voice from off to Paul's right.

Then, another voice off to the left said, "Save yourself by coming down from there on your own... *IF* you are the Son of God."

The crowd broke out in laughter. Another voice from behind mocked him even more. "Others he can save, but himself he can not." The crowd roared with laughter once again.

Paul heard Jesus again say something, slowly and painfully.

"Father... please forgive these... for... they don't... understand... what it is... that they... are doing."

Paul was shaking with horror. He had read in the history books in school about crucifixion as a form of execution, but never quite understood it—the preparation of the victims; the beatings and whippings; the unbelievably cruel and barbaric method of nailing their hands and ankles to the beams; the public mockery and humiliation; the sickening way the masses found so much humor and satisfaction in it all.

It was bad enough that he was here, in a land and time so far from his own. But to actually witness this, and see a man whom he knew, and had direct contact with only hours before, one so gentle and tender... loving and caring... die such a slow and painful death. He would *never* be the same again.

As Paul muddled through these thoughts, the skies grew very dark from storm clouds off in the distance. Again, Jesus spoke, and his pain and suffering was growing even more profound.

"Father... Father... why... have... you... forsaken... me?"

Indeed, Paul thought, why had he been forsaken? Jesus had done nothing wrong. And he was the main attraction, being executed between what? Thieves? That was what he had heard from the crowd.

Just then, one of the thieves spoke, addressing Jesus in the same kind of painful voice. "Give it up, already... save yourself... if you are the Messiah... and us too... just shut up."

Then, the other thief spoke, arguing with the first. "You shut up... don't you fear God... even as you die? Can't you see... He is innocent... of any crimes?"

He then turned to Jesus. "Jesus, sir... please... remember me... in your... kingdom... to come."

Jesus turned his head to address him, a faint smile on his face. "I promise you... friend... today... you will be with me... in paradise."

A few moments later, Jesus yelled out in agony. Paul saw the life begin to leave his body, just as he had only a short time before, when Britne...

"It... is... finished," Jesus said. Then after a pause, "Father... into... your... hands... I... commit... my... spirit."

And he died, his head falling to his chest.

At that moment the skies broke forth in terrible thunder and lightning, and a powerful earthquake shook the foundations of the earth. Boulders shattered and the ground shifted and moved like a great earthen tsunami. This went on for a good sixty seconds. Women were screaming, and soldiers were falling to the ground for protection.

Paul's heart stopped right then, and fear gripped his entire body. He lay flat to the ground, holding on for dear life, looking up at Jesus' dead body on the cross. *Surely,* he thought, *he is the Son of God.*

As the quake calmed, some of the soldiers that had been chasing Paul spotted him again. At the same time, he spotted them, and the chase was on once more. He took off running, harder than he had ever run in his life.

In the distance he saw a river, with trees and rocks abounding. If he could only make it to that river, that water—that refuge. It was raining, and the water was refreshing to his face. He kept running, and running, and running. Looking over his shoulder again, he saw that the soldiers had fallen behind, and some of them had even turned around. He pressed on, sensing for the first time that he was about to find freedom from the demons that had chased him for so very long.

And he ran, toward the river, toward the water… *toward freedom!*

REDEMPTION

Paul was sitting on the river bank, listening to the *Damascus Road* songs again. More than ever, the songs on this CD spoke to him in the deepest and most personal way. Memories filled his mind of the morning Steve had given it to him, the cynicism with which he had received it, the first time he had played it while cruising on his motorcycle. Little did he know then just how much the Lord would use those songs to change his heart and his mind. Little did he know how much they would mean to him now.

So, he sat there and listened once again, with a renewed peace in his life…

I Am the way to the Father.
I Am the path to eternity.
I Am a guiding hand to lead you
A shining light to your feet…

I Am……………Do do do do
I Am………………………………
I Am……………Do do do do
I Am………………………………

I Am the truth in time uncertain,
put your faith in my Name:
For all that is written,
it there for you to gain….

*I Am the life and the essence
of existence in a world of pain.
I hold all things together.
I am here today.*

*I Am..................Do do do do
I Am......................................
I Am..................Do do do do
I Am here today.
I Am here today.
I Am here today.*

He removed the headphones from his ears and placed the CD player on the ground next to him. He now understood. Why had it taken so long, and so much suffering—so much loss and pain—for him to grasp the truth about this man? After all, it wasn't a complicated message. Not at all. Quite frankly, it was the simplest of messages, and could be summarized in one word: Love.

Slipping the knife from its sheath, he began shaving, trying to sort out the abundance of feelings and questions he still had inside his heart. Yes, he understood the truth about Jesus, but there was so much more he needed help with. He chuckled again, thinking about how he tended to make things so difficult, so confusing, so convoluted.

The trickling of the water as it flowed ever so slowly had always had a soothing effect on Paul, and he was getting lost in his thoughts when his hand slipped and he nicked himself.

"Ow—Jesus!" he said.

"Yes?" came a voice from behind him.

Paul jumped a few feet forward, into the water. Struggling to pull his gun, he found himself splashing around under the water.

Seemingly out of nowhere, a hand reached down into the water, and lifted him up as he was gasping for air.

He opened his eyes, and there he was, standing in front of him. He could only stare at him in amazement. Right there in front of him! He was tongue-tied, and didn't know what to say, fumbling with words like he was a little child.

"You're dead," Paul said incredulously. "I mean, I saw you on the cross."

Jesus nodded at him. "I died, yes. But now," he said with a huge smile, "I live!"

"But... but... ?" Paul was too shocked to speak.

"You called me?" Jesus asked.

"What?"

Jesus touched Paul's face where he had cut himself. "Just a moment ago. You called my name."

Paul touched his face, and looked into Jesus' eyes. "Oh, sorry."

Jesus raised his hand, as if to say "*I forgive you*," then told Paul, "Call on me at any time, just not in vain. It hurts. Hey, that's easy to remember... call me in vain... cause me pain. I like it." Jesus smiled at Paul, a smile of love.

Paul paused a moment. "I saw you *die* on the cross."

"Yes, you did."

"And now... you're here."

"Yes, I am."

"But... how?" Paul had to know.

Jesus spoke to him firmly but gently. "Open your heart, Paul, and you'll understand. It's why I was born, why I lived... to die."

"Why?" Paul asked, confused.

"Sin, my brother... Sin," Jesus answered. "It's the only way back to the Father. You only have to believe and repent. Listen, you need to understand something very important. I love you. Always have, and always will. I died for you, on that cross. You, Tony, Missy, Britne—everyone. I knew you before you were born, and was intimately involved in your conception. Don't ever forget that, even if you think you don't *feel* my love, because true love is not a feeling. It's a choice, an act of your will… a way of life. Have faith, because my love never fails. I'm always here for you, to talk to, to lean on, to laugh with. Always. And this anger and bitterness you hold inside, Paul, you *must* let it go, before it kills you."

"How?" Paul asked. "I don't know how."

"Forgive, Paul. Forgive… and be forgiven. Like love, it, too, is a choice. Let go of your own selfishness. Accept me, follow me, and I will accept you."

"How?" Paul persisted. "How? It's all so… difficult."

"Not really. It's simple, and it's possible," Jesus explained. "It still comes down to this one fundamental thing, Paul. You must make a choice. Whom will you follow? Whom will you serve? With my Spirit in your heart, all things are possible. But it's *only* with my Spirit. There are many paths, but I… I AM the *only* way to the Father, and his Kingdom. Choose your eternity, one with me, or one without me. It's really that simple. I love you, Paul, truly I do. Accept that love, and my Peace will be with you."

They looked into each other's eyes for a long moment. Then Jesus hugged Paul intensely, and it seemed he would never let go.

Jesus turned and began to walk away, and Paul started to run out of the water after him.

"Wait!… Please… Jesus!"

Paul slipped on the bank of the river, fell and hit his head, and lost consciousness.

SAVED

Paul came to, and saw the siren lights and heard the radio chatter in the air. He felt himself being lifted and loaded onto a gurney.

"Welcome back, my friend. It's a miracle you're alive," said a paramedic as he strapped Paul to the gurney.

"Wha… what's happening… where am I?" Paul asked him as he was being loaded into the ambulance. As the doors were being shut, he saw Tony, barely distinguishable in the blur he was experiencing.

THOUGHTS

Sometimes dreams do come true, but not always the way we would expect. When they do come true, our view of life can change dramatically. What we thought was reality turns out to be the opposite. What we thought was truth, well... just turns out to be another lie. Somehow, we've got to test everything we believe. To do that, we need to know what the truth really is...

EPILOGUE

A year had passed since that time in his life. *Damascus Road* had been rebuilt, and the parking lot was about half full of cars, with others pulling in. The club was more popular than ever, filling every night and still adhering to the policies and values set forth by its late founder.

Inside, Paul was walking around amongst the people. He exchanged waves with a few people as he walked by, and finally settled onto a stool at the end of the bar, near the front door. A short moment later, Tony walked into the club.

Paul saw him enter, and stood up, not sure exactly how to handle this. Tony headed his way, stopping about five feet from him. Neither of them moved, and Paul began to get nervous as they stood there, looking into each other's eyes.

"Hi, Tony," Paul said cautiously.

Tony had tears forming in his eyes. "So, big brother… here we are."

"Yeah," Paul said, pausing for a moment. "What about it, bro?"

Tony looked around, astonished, and settled his gaze on the large tablets of the Ten Commandments above the bar. "I didn't think you would finish it."

"The club?" Paul asked, knowing exactly what Tony meant.

"What else?"

"I had to do it," Paul asserted. "*Someone* had to do it."

"It just had to be you, though?"

Paul smiled at him. "This is who I am, now, and you helped me get here."

Tony turned his head away. "Yeah… whatever."

They stared at each other for a moment longer, then Tony turned abruptly to walk out.

Paul reached out to him as he did. "Tony!"

He stopped, but didn't turn around.

Paul continued, smiling, "I love you with all of my heart, bro… with *all* my heart… but I love Jesus even more. You can blow this place up a hundred times, and even kill me, but neither of those two facts will change… ever!"

Tony turned his head ever so slightly, but not enough for Paul to see the tear rolling down his face, or the slight smile forming on his lips.

"I love you, too, big brother," he said under his breath, and then walked out the door.

THOUGHTS

Once we've learned the truth... all we have to do... is make a choice.

AND A NEW BEGINNING

The band on stage was the same band that played that first night Paul came to *Damascus Road*, and the same band that recorded the CD. He watched them, as the singer addressed the crowd inside.

"This next song is about choices," he said. "Choices of the heart, and for our future. It's called 'Reach Out.'"

The crowd cheered as the song began. Paul listened intently to the melancholy acoustic melody, taking in the words and remembering where he'd come from, and who he used to be.

> *Reach out, don't be afraid to hold my hand.*
> *Come along, I'll take you to*
>   *the promised land.*
> *But you've got to believe in me,*
> *You can't go on questioning*
> *All that I've ever said to you.*
>
> *Step out, don't be afraid to walk with me.*
> *The promises I've made to you I guarantee.*
> *Nothing that you say or do*
> *Will change how much that I Love you*
> *I proved that by hanging on a tree.*
>
> *For three days I lived a life of hell for you.*
> *Burning in the pain caused by all you do.*
> *I've paid the price for all you've done.*
> *And I'm coming back to take you home,*
> *Away from this life of abuse.*

So, Rise up and take a stand, it's not too late.
Choose, this day, to follow me through
    Heaven's Gate.
Don't be fooled by all the lies,
I am the Way to Truth and Life.
Only through me can you be saved.

The guitarist broke off on a beautiful, melodic lead, and Paul stood there lost in his thoughts. They were soon interrupted by Missy, who had just walked up to him. Mark was with her, and she was holding a little baby.

"Paul… Paul?" she asked.

"Oh, hi sis… I was just listening to the band."

"Well," she said, "we were in the neighborhood and thought we'd stop in and say hello." She turned to her baby. "Joshua, baby… say hello to uncle Pauly."

Paul took the baby from her. "Hey there, dude." He kissed the baby very lovingly. "What a stud."

They all laughed

Mark asked, "Hey, was that Tony we passed out on Damascus Road?"

Paul was quiet for a moment, then said softly, "Yeah… that was Tony."

"Is everything okay?" Missy asked. "Are *you* okay?"

Paul smiled a huge grin at her, and to himself. "Babe, I have a new life, and I've never felt better."

They smiled at each other, and Paul turned to look at the crowd. They were cheering the start of a new song, one he knew well, and one he knew was going to speak to many of the people in the club. He listened to the words, knowing they were meant for him.

Changes are comin'
I feel it in the air…

In the last days, God says, I will pour out my spirit on all people. Your sons and daughters will prophesy, your young men will see visions...

Acts. 2:17

FINAL THOUGHTS

This story is dedicated to The One and Only, the true Son of God, Jesus Christ. Without Him, there is no hope, no promise, and no future. Everything created was done so by Him, through Him and for Him. It's my hope that this story has served to bring you, the reader, closer to the realization that each and every one of us needs Him. Our dreams and hopes are futile and empty without first coming to acknowledge Jesus as Lord and Savior, and submitting our will and life to the Father. Jesus died for one purpose—to bring each and every one of us into reconciliation with our Father and Creator. Thank you, Lord Jesus, for loving us enough to die for us, knowing that so many would choose to reject you. This project is for you, and for all who ultimately choose you.

To the following people, the deepest and most heartfelt gratitude is expressed: Mark, Bob and Greg—your support and friendship is priceless; Rachel—nurture your special gift from the Lord; PePe'—you stepped up to the plate, and knocked one out of the park; Trace—you flipped the dirt, and took part in a miracle; Jesse & Gaby, the Weathermen—the rain stopped because of you; Pops—the torch has been passed on; Kids—dreams do come true, so find your own and never stop believing; Finally... ReRe... more often than not, the Lord works His miracles through the tender and obedient hearts of His children. Thank you for everything.

TATE PUBLISHING & *Enterprises*

Tate Publishing is committed to excellence in the publishing industry. Our staff of highly trained professionals, including editors, graphic designers, and marketing personnel, work together to produce the very finest books available. The company reflects the philosophy established by the founders, based on Psalms 68:11,

"THE LORD GAVE THE WORD AND GREAT WAS THE COMPANY OF THOSE WHO PUBLISHED IT."

If you would like further information, please call
1.888.361.9473
or visit our website
www.tatepublishing.com

TATE PUBLISHING & *Enterprises*, LLC
127 E. Trade Center Terrace
Mustang, Oklahoma 73064 USA